When
Women Rule

When Women Rule

stories by
Austin Clarke

McClelland and Stewart

Financial assistance of the Canada Council and the
Ontario Arts Council towards the publication of this
book is gratefully acknowledged.

The Canadian Publishers
McClelland and Stewart Limited
25 Hollinger Road, Toronto M4B 3G2

Canadian Cataloguing in Publication Data

Clarke, Austin
    When women rule: stories
ISBN 0-7710-2129-1
I. Title.
PS8505.L36W48 1985 C813'.54 C85-098324-X
PR9199.3.C54W48 1985

49,780

Typography and assembly by The Literary Service,
Toronto, Ontario

Printed and bound in Canada by Webcom Limited

For Ria Jean McMurtry

Acknowledgements

"The Collector" was broadcast on CBC's "Anthology," 1965.

"Give It a Shot" was published in the *Journal of Caribbean Studies*, Vol. 2, No. 1, Spring 1981; and broadcast on CBC's "Anthology," 1982.

"Griff!" was published in *When He Was Free and Young and He Used to Wear Silks*, Little, Brown and Company, Boston, 1973.

"Doing Right" was broadcast on CBC's "Anthology," 1984.

"On One Leg" was broadcast on CBC's "Anthology," 1967.

Also by Austin Clarke

The Survivors of the Crossing

Amongst Thistles and Thorns

The Meeting Point

Storm of Fortune

The Bigger Light

When He Was Free and Young and
   He Used to Wear Silks

The Prime Minister

Growing Up Stupid Under the Union Jack

Contents

The Collector

BY CHANCE NICK SAW THE LANDLADY GET OFF
the Sherbourne bus three doors from the house. He
snatched up his coat, his hat, his old shopping bag lined
with three others, and slipped through the side door. The
landlady was coming for the rent. He was thirteen weeks in
arrears. She had given him four o'clock today, Saturday, as
the deadline. But she had come early, to sit in the hallway
like a lifeguard, to watch and catch the slippery roomers.

Shuffling along the weary laneway of blackened winter
palings to reach Wellesley Street a block of safety away,
he could feel the arctic in the wind climbing his trousers
starched with urine and vomit. Nick had forgotten his
underwear. But it was more than forgetfulness. Last night
he had tottered home drunk from the Selby Hotel after
twenty-three draughts of fifteen-cents-apiece beer. He had
spent three hours begging strangers for twenty of them
because the clientele was changing like transients and
prostitutes in the rooming houses on Sherbourne. Some of
the Friday-night payday drinkers despised him, some
pitied him and some threw quarters and dimes on the salt-
sprinkled table top. He had vomited on his clothes on the
street, and had narrowly escaped the cruising eyes of a
police car which drew abreast just as another car stalled.

The car hid him from the cruiser. That was five hours ago. It was now seven o'clock. The landlady did not sleep late when rent was due.

Nick tried to remember the events of last night. But to think on an empty stomach, in the cold and with a spinning head. . .well, he had to think about rent: seven dollars which he had promised to pay first thing this morning at nine.

He had pleaded with the landlady for ten minutes on the pay phone in the hallway.

"And if not at nine, at four the latest, Mr. Evans. I don't intend sitting here all day!"

Last night, wondering how to get the money, he went into the Selby and saw Indian Johnson, who loaned him two dollars from his part-time car-washing wage of eight dollars a day. But before getting up, he helped Indian drink out the remaining six, and then spent the loan on Indian and himself. "You just loaned me two. I loan you back two. Now we square. Right?"

Indian Johnson grabbed him and hissed, "Who say so?" Rubbing the circulation back into his neck, Nick conceded, "All right, all right. I was only joking, Indian." And that transaction was forgotten.

On this cold morning, before the garbage trucks crawled out like white cockles, he was retracing memories along his favourite, fruitful route, searching for bottles. He had to be early to find his Pepsi, Coke, Teem and ginger ale bottles, which were among the most valuable empties.

It was following an attack of pneumonia in 1964, and the beginning of an arthritic tenseness in his arms, that Nick first experienced the taste of chronic hardship. He lost his job washing cars in a semi-automatic car wash because his limbs were suddenly like the Tin Man's and he no longer was the whizzing wizard of shine and tone among cars; and because too often he got to work too late, too drunk.

He never impressed the manager that he had to drink a lot to help the pain a little, to soothe the unbearable stings that rambled through his legs and his right arm. Nick never discovered why the needles of torment didn't enter his left arm. "If only I was a south-paw, why, I could lick that job!"

He hadn't worked that year until late May, when hunger and the exhaustion of friends from whom he tricked nickels with, "Mister, spare-a-dime-for-a-cuppa-karfee?" drove him to the verge of welfare, to experiment with his body; and working as a delivery man in the Parliament Street slums, tramping over lawns and broken bottles, dog filth and human filth, old mattresses and forgotten shoes and hand-bags, to stuff letterboxes with samples of Dial soap which "kills bacteria and prevents odours." Nick threw most of them on rotting porches or left them in the yards, forgotten like advertisements for pizza and Chinese food. And scarcely had he received his wages from the distributing company when he traded his job for draught beer and potato chips in the Chez Moi, and cursing "them fugging kooks" (the Canadiens) who "beat the pants off Toronto Maple Leafs" in the hockey championships recently. But his money ran out faster than his hatred for French Canada. And after a few "loans" — a dollar here, seventy-five cents there, and "Buy me one, mister?" — he was plunged into the gutters of Toronto, searching for empty wine bottles. He found them in laneways, parking lots and garbage cans.

In those collecting days he drank wine: cheap, throat-corroding wine. The value of wine bottles was high as the wages of sin. But one night he and his friend Indian Johnson parked in a cold car beside the car wash where Indian worked (where Nick used to work) and they drank wine and talked; and drank; and talked about boxing, that "Cassius Clay gonna burst Floyd's kisser"; and they drank some more, and talked some more about Clay's left jab

("Goddamn, Indian, I see myself now with Clay's left, *wham!* right in a cop's face! *Whomm!*"); and they drank until they couldn't talk anymore, until the yellow cruiser with two policemen found them early that Sunday morning in the little 1928 Model T Ford that was on display advertising weddings; their bodies in the thickness of friendship and vomit, and joined by some sort of homosexual bond.

Nick said afterwards he smelled alcohol on the breath of the ruddy-faced policeman who drove the cruiser. Nick was charged with being drunk in a public place. And Indian was beaten and sobered up by the other, greying policeman before they reached the station. And then they took Indian home, to the doorstep of the house where his Blue Cross identification slip said he lodged. From that night Nick's mind turned against drinking wine and collecting wine bottles — and policemen.

Now, before the dogs awoke, before the hearses of garbage trucks, before Indian or his friends could crawl from the drunken haphazard sleep under the stairs of basements (three weeks last winter Nick slept in the furnace room of a hotel before the Greek waiter who sneaked him there in exchange for his body grew tired of it and then beat him), before the yawning first passengers of nurses going to hospitals, you can see Nick in a too-large brown winter coat, dark glasses ("Never let a man see the look in your eye, Indian, never!"), shoes as large as a clown's, shuffling north along Church Street to search for the symptoms of last night's illicit drinking and happiness and love and sex in parked alleyways. Nick knows the city better than the mayor because he knows the city's garbage.

"Ah, a bottle!" It is glimmering like sun and snow by a post in the parking area of a supermarket. Nick shuffles up on feet that have no arches, his arches having fallen years ago from marching in the war, from walking the halls of the university where he worked as a porter-messenger

14

before they found him with a philosophy student in a telephone booth in the basement, a breath away from the liniment and sweat of the men's gymnasium. So here he is now, archless, a man with a fallen past and present, broken recently when he jobbed one week as an orderly at the Doctors' Hospital.

"Five cents! A wine bottle, goddamn! Need a washing, though." There is a note inside. Nick pounds the bottle against his palm; a small black cockroach crawls out and touches his skin. He drops the bottle and it crashes, all five cents' worth. "Goddamn!" He stomps his foot like a ton of slab on the cockroach, three times, although it's already dead. "Bugger! Bugger! Bugger!" He wipes away the stain of the cockroach. He kicks away the crystals of the bottle; and then he remembers the note written on a double-lined half page. Norman, I am not making no more fun with you. I have taken the baby to my mother. You can find me there, if you want me. Elaine.

Nick worried about Elaine and the baby. Would Norman chicken out? Would Norman go to Elaine's mother's place? ("Mother-in-laws is bitches!") And he wondered whether Elaine left Norman because he was spending all his wages on wine and sin, instead of getting milk for the baby. Was the room and the baby cold?. . . But he shrugged these thoughts away because he had to look for more bottles and find a storekeeper willing to buy them. "Some o' them bastards, they think they own this city!"

He was now out for twenty minutes, and not a bottle. So he scoured the parking area like a vacuum cleaner and found three more bottles near a pile of cigarette butts and some balls of Kleenex stained with lipstick. He put the bottles into his shopping bag and the butts into his coat pocket. "Gonna be a great day!"

He saw himself in a short while sitting in his room, his rent paid, emptying his butts into the old Macdonald cigarette tin which Indian had given him for Christmas three Christmases ago when the tin was full; and waiting for Indian to call, as he said he would, to share the bottle of Seagrams VO which Indian "had found" in a car at the car wash.

But he couldn't put Norman and Elaine and the baby out of his mind. You find some strange things in empties, eh? You could almost tell what kind of person throws away a bottle. In anger or hiding from the police. And even the way a person feels. Now look at that VO bottle I picked up last Sunday by the Christadelphians' place on Asquith Avenue. Why, that bottle even had a French leather in it, and the stuff was in it too! Betcha they had a ball! Were they Christadelphians, though?

And once Nick found a small Canada Dry bottle in a garbage pail near an apartment on Jarvis Street. And when he looked into it and saw the bills rolled inside, he almost dropped it. It took him ten shaking minutes to get the money out of the bottle. Twenty-one one-dollar bills! It saddened him to think it might belong to a pensioner, probably an old woman. He knew old women who kept money in bottles. He thought of returning it. . .But I would have to press every damn buzzer in this apartment building. I ain't no damn postman! He was glad there were so many names and buzzers, and no address in the bottle. He kept the money.

That morning he collected no more bottles; he didn't remember his landlady and he didn't remember his rent. He and Indian Johnson found Cabbie, the bootlegger, and spent the money on a bottle of Canadian Club plus three bottles of wine.

"Indian, when I spotted them dollars, what you think I did first?" "You whistled?" Indian said. "I say *God!*" They had just finished the whisky. "First time in years that I think 'bout God. But! One man losses is another man's profits." Indian remained unimpressed. "Wine taste good, Nick Evans. If old woman lost money and Nick Evans find it, finders is keepers, I say. I see wine in this glass, not a old woman. Not even money. *Wine!* It's your fortune. Look, we sitting here like kings, like chiefs watching football. King Nick and Chief Indian Johnson. Man wants no better life, Nick Evans."

When Indian called him Nick Evans, he did it derisively. In order to fight discrimination when he was an insurance salesman for Manufacturers Life just after the war, Nick had anglicized his name into Evans. But the benefits that were to follow never appeared. At least Indian never saw them. And he told Nick once, "I tell you something. I's a Indian with the name Johnson. You's a foreigner with the name Evans. In a way we's brothers, eh?"

"You want to know something, Indian? I's a man fifty-five years old. You must be the same age, give or take a year. Me and you sitting here, goddamn, drinking out this twenty-one dollars, and perhaps right at this minute a old woman might be out there crying for this money as I raise this glass to my. . .*burrrrp!*. . .head. And something else. Listen. This twenty-one bucks could pay my rent for three weeks. But I didn't even think of rent. Same way you didn't think of the old woman who's the rightful owner o' this money. If I had paid the blasted rent, why, if not next week, well, the *next* week I would still be looking for more rent *and* wine. And when we drink this wine, as we intend to, I still need more wine *and* rent!"

Indian took a large mouthful and said, "I glad you's a man of wisdom, Nick Evans. You didn't have to invite me, but you invite me nevertheless. That's kindness. But why talk 'bout rent or the old woman or the landlady? Drink the fugging wine!"

"Indian, you know, you's a goddamn genius!"

They watched the entire football game, drinking and

not saying a word. Then Nick said, "Indian, you know something? When I found this twenty-one bucks I felt I had my whole fortune, future, in front o' my eyes. Why, it isn't once or twice but many times I lays down on this bed where we sitting, watching that bastard Jimmy Brown chew up that New York line, and I dream that I'm searching under trees for empties and I can't find one lousy empty. But I spot a quarter, and the more I search, the more there's quarters coming at me. Like water springing up. And the more quarters I throw in my bag, the more quarters coming. Why, last week I had this same dream. And I had to say to myself, Nick Evans. . ."

"You's a fugging man!" Indian said. "One day you will be rich as a millionaire. It's in your stars. So keep searching for empties. If not this sunset, then tomorrow's sunrise."

They had watched television until the seven-o'clock news came on and found them asleep, as the television snored about the above-average fatalities in Canada that holiday weekend.

Nick emerges from his reminiscences and spots three coke bottles beside a bus stop. He hurries, charles-shuffling, and is about to cross the street against a red light. "But what the hell?" In his imagination he's picking up the empties when a boy on a bicycle roars around the corner, shouting, "Hey! Rocket Richard! He shoots, he *scores*!" He looks at Nick, smiles and asks, "You see that, mister?"

In the middle of the road, transfixed by hate, Nick sees the bottles crash against the opposite bank. He watches the boy manoeuvring off the saddle like a snake, punching the pedals, zigzagging to overtake the wind. "You *bastard*!" Nick shouts into the wind and walks on.

On and on, up one street on one side, down the same street on the other side, on and on, walking, looking and finding coke bottles, five cents, need a washing. . . hey! half dozen beer empties, six more and I got a quarter! And kicking a useless whisky bottle back into the gutter of evil.

Searching with his left foot (he always poked that foot under bushes) and occasionally getting it polished with the brown vaseline of a dog's defecation. "Shit!" But even defecation can't deter him this morning. So, as always, he shines his left shoe in the snow and shuffles along on his right foot, pounding the numbness out of his left.

All of a sudden women and men appear around him, holding scarves and hats with their early-to-rise unskilled calloused hands. Nick sees them in the blowing snow, waiting for transportation.

'Twas a time when he too was working, not stunted by the abuses of fate and necessity or shamed by this collecting of embarrassing empty bottles. Nick glares at the people, hates them and buries them in his wishes. 'Twas a time when he too would be standing, thawing, waiting at this snowman corner for a taxi to take him to Manufacturers Life. 'Twas a time when the skin on his face wasn't peeling like a lizard's; before wine skidded blood to his face in a perpetual sunset of red and made him slip; before the arthritis; before the pneumonia; before the Greek waiter ate his body like a banana and threw away the peeling.

But now, Nick, a blind man is beside you. He's tapping his long white eye on the sidewalk. Nick sees him crossing the street outside the double-lined crosswalk, tapping his way into the rushing Italian construction traffic. He doesn't touch the man's arm to say, Look out! The rushing panel truck doesn't see the white stick through the windshield that has winter on it. And then, brakes scream. *"Madre! Coñon! Madre!"*

The blind man jerks to attention. And stumbles. Men and women thinking of work turn their faces. The blind man re-taps to the sidewalk; and in the seconds of guilt and hate and hushed pity, he stands beside Nick. He smells Nick's presence again and turns to him and says, "You can't see?"

Shuffling away from the blind man, he approaches the

insurance section: tall buildings of granite and glass that have the best Christmas trees and decorations and front lawns in the whole city, with their double indemnities of ugliness and vaults of money. Among them is Manufacturers where, had this morning been January 3, 1946, he would be heading. . . "'Twas a time, Indian, when I would be taking the elevator to the ninth floor. . ."

A streetcar inspector, greying like a mouse in his uniform, stealthily drinks the last two gulps of a small bottle of Pepsi and looks around to see who sees, to see where to put the bottle. Nick holds out his shopping bag. The inspector hops onto the moving streetcar, and just before the doors swallow him, he looks back. "Nick?" he asks. He recognizes him. "*Nick!*"

Nick has recognized him too. He has taken an empty bottle from the man who beat up Indian Johnson that night when they were drunk in the Model T. Six months afterwards, this man beat up a West Indian nightclub owner and was dismissed from the police force under the alibi of "heart condition," and not, as one newspaper suggested, "because of police brutality against Toronto blacks."

Remembering the man, Constable Broda van Pistle, ex, Nick felt spit in his throat, and the more he relived that violent night, the more he shuddered and the thicker the spit congealed. He could not even get it out. But he did the only remaining dignified thing he could do: he searched in his bag among the empties for that Pepsi bottle, and when at last his shaking hands grabbed it, he aimed it at the middle of the street. . .but a police cruiser was passing and the eyes and the street were watching.

Instead, he went into a restaurant. The manager growled, "What d'you want, mister?" Nick, wanting the warmth of the restaurant and a coffee but having no money, said, "I have some empties. . ." The manager, a Greek with thick eyelashes and a thick mustache that made him look tough, was waiting. Nick hated Greeks even more than policemen, for Greeks would tell him, "Drink up!" though they saw his soup was hot. "I have some empties. . ."

Something like the blood of anger came into the manager's face. "*Git!*" he screamed. And shuffling out, all the time with the manager mumbling, "Decent people in business eat their lunch here, mister!. . .you smell. . ." Nick saw that the clock said something to twelve.

"'Twas a time during the war when Toronto was a hell-uva place. Even after the war. I could spend maybe fifty bucks drinking with a broad, and another twenty on a meal in the King Eddy on a Friday night. 'Twas a time when to lose seventy bucks in a crap game was *nothing*, a time when this goddamn country was free from DP's, with no fugging Greeks, when this country was *clean*. . ." But now all he can hear are the sirens in the Greek's scream, "*Git!*"

He shuffled out to the back streets among the broken men and women like himself, where he knew he wasn't conspicuous. The scream went with him, like a pneumatic drill in the hands of a new Italian immigrant, *git-git-git!*

Time was against him now. It was past twelve-thirty. The landlady had bellowed over the telephone, "Four, Mr. Evans! And *cash!* Not a minute later. If it isn't in my hand by four. . ." and she had left the rest of the threat to his imagination.

Nick knew how cruel she was. She had thrown his clothes in the snow one night when his rent was two weeks late. That night he came home tottering, arm in arm with Indian, and he saw his Japanese transistor radio growing out of the snow, its batteries probably frozen but still miraculously playing *I Want to Hold Your Hand*. . . Everything he owned was in public view. And he was so ashamed that Indian was present. "One thing about this country,

Indian, it's free. And it belongs to we, we Canadians," he had told him during an argument at the Selby.

Nick had sat in the snow on the steps and cried, and called his landlady "this fugging Kraut!" Indian knew his sorrow. "Goddamn, we was fighting them bastards in the last war. And now Canada letting them into this country, *my* fugging country! And they're treating me this way? But, Indian, far's I's concerned, war still on! And I still killing Germans. I even dream the landlady was one o' them. Why, only last night, thinking about the rent, I dreamed I had strangle the bitch. And now a German woman could throw my clothes and my thirty-nine dollars in transistor on the fugging sidewalk? Ain't we Canadians, Indian?" Indian had picked up the transistor, changed the station and said, "I's a Indian, Nick Evans." Nick kicked his clothes into the road. A car passed over them, and then he picked them up. The next five days were days collecting bottles to raise the rent, before the landlady gave him back his key. Since that time, Nick made a point of not acquiring too many possessions. He had learned his humiliating lesson.

Now he stopped beside a garbage pail which gave up one large Canada Dry bottle. It was time to check his collection, and when he did, it was worth fifty cents. And the time was two o'clock. "Goddamn! Sweating off my ass this whole morning, and for what? Fifty lousy cents!" He thought of spending it at the Chez Moi; but rent first, Nick. And Indian, that bastard, might be there. He decided on the Selby as a better place to hide in a corner with a draught of beer. Indian might be there too. And I not spending *one* penny on that bastard. Not today, Mister Indian!

Bottles were scarce for this grown man, a war veteran, a Canadian, sniffling and shuffling in the chilly wind, up and down like a dog. A kind of open-air imprisonment locked him in: he thought he heard the manager's scream — *git-git-git!* — abuses and pebbles thrown at a dog poised to pee on somebody's lawn.

"I feel like a goddamn dog!" He was now crawling instead of shuffling, and his shoulders drooped. The arthritis in his arms became heavy, and his legs were painless logs. He was struggling not to hang his arms too loosely, not to be a spaniel! But he was dog-tired. He came to somebody's front steps, brushed off the snow and sat down. But as he was about to pour out his heavy sighs in exchange for winter air, a head above screamed, *"Scoot, bugger!"* He looked up. He stood up. And when he looked down to walk on the tricky steps, a police cruiser, eternal as the poverty in this slum, was standing silently beside him. The face that looked at him was a ruddy face. "Git in, Nick!" It was a command, and possibly an arrest. "Git! Come on!" And Nick got in.

Time and its meaning were now slipping from him. He did not recognize where the cruiser was taking him. He did not think of the charge to be laid against him. He did not regret being picked up. He looked forward to being jailed. He was too tired and too cold. And after many turns, which in his normal hazed sobriety Nick would have known like the bottom of a beer glass, the cruiser stopped and the officer said, "Okay, Mack. Git out." And Nick got out.

Beside him was a mountain of empty bottles: Canada Dry ginger ale, Teem, coke, Pepsi and one marked Wink. All sorts of bottles. His dream had come true: searching for bottles and finding quarters! But this time, instead of quarters, it was bottles; and although each bottle wasn't worth one quarter, still there were enough for three weeks' rent. He thought of Indian's words, *Keep searching for empties. If not this sunset, then tomorrow's sunrise.* "Indian, we gonna have a ball tonight! Goddamn! There's more empties here than whores in the Selby. I *knew* this was a lucky morning."

Nick was overjoyed. It was only three-fifteen. Time was with him again. He took up a Pepsi bottle, held it close to his eyes and looked and saw clearly many young generations of teenagers, swinging and singing to "get with it" and "stay alive" — for this, goddammit, Nick, is the fugging Pepsi generation!

"Get with it, Indian!" And he screamed. And he started to put the bottles into his shopping bag.

He was standing by the green paling of a construction site. And a crane marked Teperman, boasting with bright orange, was swinging debris from the ground and depositing it on the building. Nick wasn't sure whether Teperman was building the wreckage or wrecking the building.

His shopping bag could hold only thirty bottles. The bag was very heavy for him to carry. He didn't know how far the nearest grocery store was. He started counting, figuring out exactly how much money the bottles were worth: find a drug store or take these bottles to the nearest... No, count them first, then to Starkman's, that big, never-closing place on Bloor. The beer bottles could be dropped off at Brewers Retail. Goddamn, a lotta liquor tonight! Yah-hooo! Indian! Wah-wah-wah!

There were three hundred and eighty-two empties, five whisky bottles which he smashed immediately, and thirteen wine bottles which he discarded. "Goddamn winos!"

Spotting a taxi, he hailed it. "Starkman's!"

"Which one?" the driver asked and laughed at his own joke. There was only one in the city. "Okay, bud, *I* know."

"Instead, make it the first Dominion store we come to."

"Okay, buddy," the driver said and settled back. "You married?" Nick said never. The driver caught his remark in the mirror. "Damned lucky! Me? *Five* years. And last Friday night this broad I married left home. Took my kid to *her* mother. Ain't that a scream?" Nick thought of Elaine and her baby (was this Norman?) and of their life in that small empty wine bottle. A moment ago he was so cheerful, happy as hands rubbed together in winter. Now he was sad.

"Here!" he said to the driver and got out. He made a deal with the manager of the store and shuffled back into the cab. "Back where we come from."

"Hey! Whaddya think 'bout that nut who tried to blow up the House o' Commas?" the driver asked. "Jeez, there's more nuts living outside 999 Queen Street than inside. It woulda been fireworks like hell on Parl'ment Hill, eh? You know something, bud? There's a lotta nuts in Parl'ment too. Yeah! It shoulda been sent sky-high! That's something I woulda like to see. This country? It's shit. . ."

"I woulda *hang* that bastard. He's a fugging traitor. This's a great country. I know it. I fought in the last war and. . ."

"I woulda hang him too!" the taxi driver said. He was shocked by Nick's nationalism. Perhaps he was an under-cover cop, or a plain bum, judging by his clothes. But he knew from his profession that clothes were deceiving. "But you call *this* country great? With the Americans owning half. . . Here we are, buddy."

At first Nick could not believe this was the same laneway from which he had set out fifteen minutes ago. He looked around like a man coming out of the bad dream of a morning movie on Yonge Street to face the glare of a winter-afternoon reality. Yeah, it's here. The paling's still here. Teperman still here?. . .yeah!

The taxi driver was shouting, "Keep this meter running? Or you stopping now, Mack?"

Nick was walking along the green paling, muttering, "Three hundred and eighty-two empties I just left here. . ."

The driver was behind him, nodding as if agreeing, and

smiling because he was sure now that Nick was a nut, but a nut with money.

"Before I took your cab, I counted them myself. Three hundred and. . ."

They were standing over the broken bottles piled in a heap where Teperman had come to rest on the dot of the coffee-break hour. No dust was flying. No hammering. No thudding of iron on concrete.

At the long end of the paling an Italian was passing water. Nick bent down and picked up the bottom of a broken Canada Dry bottle. He looked at it and dropped it on the clinkering pile.

"Come *on*, Mack. Three-fifty. This's getting to be a bad day. Almost four o'clock already and I ain't made a good fare yet, and I *must* pay something to the goddamn Family Court judge. . . Come, gimme three-fifty. . .forget the tip."

"My empties. I just had them here. Three hundred and eighty-two. . ."

The taxi driver did not let him finish. He grabbed him and shook him like Teperman had been shaking the wreckage. "If you wasn't such an old bastard, I would beat the living shit outta you, you *nut*!" And he gave Nick one last punch, dropping him on the pile of broken bottles. He dragged his feet back to the taxi through the mud of the building site, then roared off with a shrieking sound.

Gazing around at his shattered rent money, pieces matching the colour of the construction paling, Nick heard the four-o'clock chime of the clock on the roof of the Manufacturers Life.

Give It a Shot

WHEN HE LEFT HOME AT SEVEN IN THE MORNING for work in the Department of Transportation, the Drivers' Examination Section, his wife was still in bed. He was glad she didn't have to lift overweight patients and empty bed-pans and watch people die today. Yesterday on her shift she watched three old women die, she told him. But today she was at home. And it pleased him. She was a wife, a housewife; and he felt like a man. He felt she was right to make him work harder and get the promotion which harder work would bring. She was right to urge him to get the part-time job at night and help them get out of the apart-ment in the Ontario housing project where they'd lived for ten years. She told him almost every morning when he left, and every evening when he got home tired from the Depart-ment of Transportation, that she wanted to live far from the welfare families and the growing number of West Indian immigrants who were moving into the project. Their cooking bothered her, she told him. She wanted to *live*. And live in a house.

Every evening she bugged him about her girl friends who had moved away already. "And some of them are even Jamaicans," she said, "so why we can't get ahead like them?"

He felt good leaving her in bed on this blood-freezing

morning. Things were tough. He needed time to think. Time to think of getting her into a better residential district. Perhaps a house in the East End, in the Beaches area where the successful people were moving. But this morning, at least, she was a wife *and* a housewife; and for the moment he was the breadwinner. He always wanted to be the breadwinner. But his job showed no prospects to finance that chauvinism. This evening when he got home he would lay his cards on the table.

He settled himself comfortably at his desk. A member of his section was home sick, so he was in charge today. He had power. He was the supervisor. Even though it was for one day, he alone would decide the fate of the applicants. He could fail them or pass them.

Before lunch he had passed five persons. One or two he could have flunked. But his wife was at home. A housewife; and he liked that. If even for one day. Yesterday he had failed ten persons. Eight of them were West Indians. His wife went to work yesterday. He had dropped her off in front of the hospital emergency entrance. And that evening she announced she had to visit her Jamaican friend, May. "She's showing me her house tonight." He had grunted. "She doesn't even have a man." That was all she said, and then she left.

A young Jamaican sits before him now. The Jamaican's head is covered by a black, red and green woollen tam-o'-shanter. He wonders if he's Jewish. And to himself he swears: I won't be letting you loose on the decent people of this city, not today, boy! His wife had slammed the apartment door, and off she went to visit May. He heard her high heels clumping down the metal stairs. And from six floors above, he heard her slam the car door. When she drove off, he thought of the repair bill. The car was old. She wanted a house: he wanted a new car. He saw the gravel skidding behind her in the parking lot, and he thought of all the greasy-haired kids he had kept off the road. He had failed them by just looking at their long hair. Thank God I had the foresight to spot them early. . .

The Jamaican sits silent and threatening in front of him. The red, black and green of his woollen cap bothers him. I'm gonna keep you waiting, buster. You people got no patience or no manners, or respect for anybody. I can't understand why you people're in so much hurry. . .

He himself was a patient man. And all his life he had respected his superiors. He was even satisfied to remain a private in the Royal Canadian Scots Reserve Guards. It took him three years to be promoted. And it would take time to save and buy a house. It had taken him so many Thursday evenings to learn the new drills and the new weapons, and he was a man who had served overseas in the last war. It was as if he was learning all over again how to master the Royal-Sal-ute-Pree-sent-Arrrms! But by God, he got it! And he had been a proud private.

Why can't this bastard have patience? And why didn't May wait a little longer to buy her house, and now have my wife bitching and bitching? He was a patient man. Last year they made him corporal. In parades, with spit and polish, even if the rain came down and made plastic of his stiff khaki uniform, he knew the virtue of patience; and respect demanded that he remain standing at attention, with only the starch of his loyalty in his stance. The Queen was visiting Toronto at the time.

He was Scottish by descent. He felt he was more loyal than the burly West Indian sergeant at the top of the line. Somewhere in a book he had seen an inscription, *James, King of England and of Scotland.* It didn't say one damn thing about King of the West Indies.

The Jamaican begins to whistle a tune. With his car key or some other key, he cleans dirt from his thumbnails. These goddamn people! You can wait till I call my wife. . .

The telephone was ringing a long time and he imagined her slipping out of bed in the long, long nightgown that made her look like a wet zebra. I never liked it, its pattern or its sleek silkiness; and now she'd be putting on her slippers and cursing him because he couldn't afford broadloom for the cold floor.

But I'm doing my best. The whole country's in a mess, and I don't have no power to change that. All these goddamn strikes, and all these immigrants writing letters to the papers complaining, and living next door. . . Doesn't she hear the goddamn phone ringing?. . . Her entire salary went to buy Canada Savings Bonds and clothes. . . She would be in the kitchen by now, standing beside the fridge with her left hand holding the red wall phone which she herself chose; and by now she's wiping the sleep out of her eyes with her right hand and trying not to smear her mascara which she sleeps with. . . What a kid! I know that kid like the back of my hand! Love her too. . .

He became lost in his thoughts, in his life, in his world, in the seductive ringing of the telephone; and the monotony of the ringing made him forget the Jamaican.

He looked up at the Jamaican and told him, "You're okay." His wife had not answered. The Jamaican sat upright, as if the two words were jabs to his stomach. "This driving permit you're getting is a great privilege. *Not* a right. This country gives you this privilege to drive. So remember that." The Jamaican smiled and said, "Right on!" He held one hand up, and in a flash the hand became a fist. "Right on!" A smile changed his face and the whitest teeth he ever saw were grinning at him; and the Jamaican walked out of the office as if he was doing the boogaloo. He liked the Jamaican, but he refused to allow himself to feel soft towards him.

All of a sudden his mind went back to the telephone call to his wife. He was sad and alone and unsure of himself.

And his insecurity made him sullen and malevolent. Another murderer, another maniac I've just let loose on society. He had given him a chance. It's a long shot, but what the hell!

The morning moved fast. He thought of a beer and a hamburger for lunch. He was obsessed by his work and by the feeling of responsibility it gave him. He called his wife two more times. He wanted to surprise her by asking her to lunch, to that place she liked so much, that place that cooked that soul-food thing. That was another thing she was getting into recently. She and those goddamn exotic foods and exotic people! Wonder if she changed her mind and went to work, after all?

He made up his mind to seriously consider the part-time job at night. Christ, I'm still better off than Bob, poor bastard.

Almost every Monday evening religiously, Bob, a neighbour on the fifth floor in his apartment building, would be sitting in his kitchen talking about the woman he married. "That bitch," Bob called her. He took refuge at the race-track. The weekends and his wife took such a toll on Bob's face, and on his performance at work, that it reflected in his luck at the track. And his losses were heaviest on the weekends. Bob used to work with him in the Department of Transportation, but when the economy took a nose dive and promotion was not forthcoming, he left this civil service job and announced he was going to make a living off the track.

No, he had nothing to complain about. The kid's okay. And that trip to the West Indies she's always bugging me about, well, if. . . "My girl friend May bought her ticket last week. . ." Well, tonight he would give her the goddamn money for the trip to Jamaica. "To the Barbados, Grenada, Antigua, South America, Cuba, any goddamn place, kid!" He could hardly wait to get home and make it up with her, doing all the things he had promised. He felt a strong spasm of love for her. She was his kid. His wife. His queen.

And when he left work, custom guided his car to a stop beside the fire hydrant in front of the main entrance of the hospital. Every day after work he would sit in this place to wait for her, and listen to the report of traffic rushing and bounding on the Don Valley Parkway, exactly where he had to travel to get home; and he would curse the city politicians and the town planners who did not give a damn about him. And here he was, protecting the city from the greasy-haired kids and immigrants who drove like maniacs on the same Don Valley.

This afternoon he remained parked illegally by the fire hydrant for a long time, thinking about the part-time job. His attention was taken up by news of accidents and traffic jams. And he would have sat longer if May hadn't come out and noticed him. "What the hell you doing here, man?" She held her bust through the window while he looked at the lace of her brassiere and smelled the enticing perfume and saw the rusty safety pin beside the flowers embroidered on her bra. "Pat, your wife not working today, man. She call in sick. She take off three days. Pat, you ain't know?" And she laughed the loud, happy laugh he had heard so often on the telephone. "So, when you coming to see my new place, eh?"

All of a sudden he couldn't smell her perfume. And he lost sight of the safety pin and the caution on the radio news about heavy traffic on the Don Valley Parkway. He wished he could catch up with that Jamaican whom he had passed. Anywhere, anyplace, anytime, I see that bastard, I'm gonna take that permit outta his goddamn hands!

The Don Valley was not crowded. He didn't know what that bastard on the radio was talking about. You can't trust any goddamn person these days! So he pressed his foot flat on the gas pedal, swung from the slow lane into the middle and straight across into the fast lane without using his indicator. A car he had just missed blew its horn. *Maniacs!* Through his rear-view mirror he saw them. He decided they were West Indians. *Goddamn maniacs! Bastards! Illegal immigrants! Fuck off!* He punched his fist on his car horn, and the frightened driver and his two passengers were left behind in a cloud of smoke and vapour.

When he reached home, he slammed on the brakes and turned off the ignition at the same time. The old car shot forward, and then died. He turned off the lights and sat for a while. He got out and looked up, trying to identify his apartment, searching among dozens for the light in his windows. His wife had placed a stubby plant on the windowsill. He hated that stubby plant. One of her nurse friends had given it to her. Those stupid bastards who're foolish enough to marry her girl friends! They need a tough bugger like me to control them. . . He did not see the plant; and he could not tell which lights were in his apartment.

Bob was in the elevator. "Months now I been telling you to give up your job and come to the races. The biggest goddamn 100 percent guaranteed investment in the world!" Two old ladies got into the elevator just before the doors closed. Bob modified his speech. "Made me a bundle today," he whispered. "Caught the Double too. Paid three bills." One old lady got out. "You're wasting time being a civil servant, Pat," he said in a louder voice. The old lady who remained was a Jamaican whom he had once seen at the track. "All these years he's working for the goddamn government. And for what?" The lady just smiled. "Me and him," he said, looking at Pat and then at the lady, "the two of us was in the war." She got off. "We fought in the goddamn war together. Where was any goddamn government? That goddamn. . ." He reached the fifth floor where he got off.

Pat remained in the humming elevator, with thoughts of

the races and winning and making a down payment on a house from those winnings. Perhaps. Perhaps he should give it a shot one of these weekends.

The carpet on which he was walking was worn bare by the treading of many feet. That's another thing wrong with this building. Too many goddamn immigrants and children. The elevator had graffiti in it. The tiles in the lobby were broken. And more than once he thought he smelled urine in the elevator.

Did I turn off my car lights? I have so many goddamn things on my mind.

A couple of times last summer he had gone to the track with Bob and made a few bucks. . . But to make a living as a racetrack tout? No, I could never do that. I'm a veteran and a public servant.

The decisions he made to withhold driving permits from West Indians and the greasy-haired kids went without publicity. Not even his supervisor raised a finger. And nobody ever took a photograph or wrote a feature story on his public spiritedness. From his training in the war and, more recently, the weekly parades at the fort down Jarvis Street, he was fashioned into a stern man. A man of discipline. I know where every penny of my paycheque goes. I can trace every goddamn penny, and if I had more, I could trace them too. . .

His key was giving him trouble. There was no light coming from under the door. Was I right about that Jamaican fellow? The door swung open and he stood facing a black apartment. He closed the door and went back into the corridor. He could smell curry. He was sure he could smell urine too. He checked the number on the door. It was his apartment. So he opened it a second time, switched on the light and stood just inside the threshold, a bit timidly, and stared at the rectangle of clean white paint where the red wall phone had been unscrewed, and at other squares and rectangles of dust and hair where furniture had once stood. And in each of these dimensions were four little dents in the softwood floor where chairs and tables, the stereo and the colour television had stood.

He's in their bedroom now. He sees the same dust and the same four sets of dents, heavier in one place and deeper because this spot represented the weight of their two bodies, tired after work, for six equally tired years, as she once told him.

The four rooms are stripped bare. But she's left the stubby plant on the windowsill in the kitchen.

The place is cold. There's one chair he finds in the kitchen. She probably remembered how tired I am at night. I need a drink. . . He opens the cupboard above the sink where he keeps his whisky. Dust and grains of sugar and flour and rice. And some black dots. The building was infested with mice and cockroaches. The kid bugged me all last week to get the super to spray this place. . . In the refrigerator, on the second shelf, is one beer and a parcel wrapped in tinfoil.

He searched for the bottle of whisky and couldn't find it. He became angry now to think that she had left a beer and had taken the bottle opener. All the cutlery was gone too. And the emptiness of the place made him hungrier than he was angry. He opened the bottle with his teeth. He sipped the beer. Something crossed his mind and he jerked his head and stood up, his thoughts racing like his old car. He rushed into the bathroom. He pushed his hand under the water tank of the toilet. When his hand touched the bundle there, he smiled and felt warmer. She had missed that. He unwrapped the Canadian flag, and from amongst its folds a gun was revealed.

Every Sunday he cleaned his gun in his parked car in the nearby park. It was a souvenir from the war. After the building became integrated, he kept it loaded. Now he dropped the Canadian flag on the hard floor and stepped over it, holding the gun in his hand like a man who is prepared for an intruder.

He's in the kitchen again. Sitting on the upright wooden chair. In one hand is the gun. In the other is the chicken leg which was in the tinfoil. He takes a large bite out of the chicken, but he could be biting her or destroying her, so ferocious is the bite. He sits facing the stubby plant.

I was a damn fool to take that chance on that goddamn Jamaican. I was a damn fool to listen to this broad. I should have put my foot down, even in her ass, and told her where to get off. I shoulda been like other men and stuffed that dead-end civil service job long time ago. . .

He got up. He watered the stubby plant with some of his beer. What am I beefing about? I've seen harder times. I was in the war. And I'm a loyal subject. I got a right to live off this goddamn country. I'm no fucking immigrant! This country owes me a goddamn living. . .

Never before had he seen so many people not at work in the middle of the day. He was at the track. No wonder there's so much unemployment! And so many West Indian immigrants! He would never have guessed from sitting at his desk in the Department of Transportation that the government had let in so many black people as immigrants. Christ, they're all here at the races!

Bob had succeeded in getting him to go to the track. Bob was a friend. He was very decent to him the night his wife left. He was surprised by his sympathy. Bob had sat with him all through that first night, looking at the stubby plant, commenting on its ugliness, and drinking the case of beer he had brought with him.

Bob turned to him now and said, "Look at these un-employed bastards, would ya?" The horses were coming through the tunnel. Bob looked over each one and made a stroke in his program. "See that one with the coloured groom? Put your money on him."

"On the groom?" He was enjoying himself.

"The horse, you bugger!"

Pat looked at the horse and then at the groom, and was sure he recognized the groom. "I had no idea there was so many goddamn Jamaicans in this racket!"

"Best goddamn grooms in the racket," Bob said, "those coloured boys are! You don't know this since you don't know horse racing, but the history of the great Kentucky Derby is the history of coloured jockeys. Now they've come from jockeys to being grooms. Let's give the 10-horse a shot."

Travelling in Bob's car on the way home that afternoon, Bob told him, "Tell ya what. . ." He was recapturing the excitement and victories he had had at the track. They were jammed in creeping traffic on the Don Valley. But he didn't care. Bob had given him three good tips, and he had won two hundred dollars, tax-free, as Bob liked to say. He had it in his pocket. Today was the third straight day he had taken off from work. Sick leave. He didn't give a damn. He would take another three days off. He didn't miss his wife.

"Tell ya what," Bob said again. "The super in our building's leaving. To go out west. They'll be looking for a super and I thought. . . So why don't you give it a shot?" Pat was finding the speeding cars fascinating. "Beats beating your brains out down at Transport," Bob told him. "Incidentally, I'm bringing a Jamaican buddy of mine to the poker game Saturday."

Next day on the way to the Woodbine racetrack, Bob told him, "Ya got it! I talked to the super, the super talked to the agent, and ya got it! Your war service came in handy. Goddamn, you're a free man now!"

They were driving in heavy holiday traffic and he was

thinking of his luck and hardly said a word. He had never had so much money before. Cash in his pockets. He didn't have to face those greasy-haired kids. . .

"Sure thing!" he said.

Bob was startled. "You all right, Pat?"

"Sure thing! The Jamaican fellow and the poker game!"

"Ya got it!" Bob said.

Why didn't I throw that broad out on her ass years ago? A new life opened its pages to him in the excitement of the *Racing Form*. He and Bob stopped taking the common entrance. Valet parking and the clubhouse became commonplace now. They stopped drinking beer and sipped scotch instead. They quickly learned the sophistication of the clubhouse. And they grinned when they won, and gritted their teeth and tried to smile when they lost, and said, "We had to give it a shot!"

One day Pat found himself standing behind a well-dressed Jamaican at the betting wicket. He had heard the man talk. And when the man moved away, the computer print-out which was still on the machine said *$900.00* in red. He told the ticket seller, "Fifty dollars to win. . .on the same horse."

"You mean the 1-horse?"

Bob had given him the 5-horse. He took the ticket. His hand was shaking. He had to give it a shot. Nervously he headed back to Bob, sitting with two scotches.

"Did ya go with me on the 5-horse?"

The same well-dressed Jamaican approached their table. He slapped Bob on the back. "That 1-horse. Look at the form in the *Form* that that 1-horse got, mastah. *Cahn't* lose!" Pat felt stronger now. "I backed it to show. Nine hundred on the motherfucker." And he left just as abruptly, to see the race.

Bob underlined in red ballpoint the 5-horse's previous performances. He showed it to Pat, who wasn't attending.

Bob then kissed his ticket. "If this 5-horse comes in at 13-to-one. . . Oh, he's the fellow, the poker fellow!. . . My trip to the Bahamas paid for. Christ, I'm gonna have me some broads in the sun!"

But Pat was committed elsewhere: that Thunderbird I put a hundred dollars on. I need only five hundred more by the weekend. Plus the rent money I borrowed which I have to put back this weekend too. . .

The first time, for almost a month, it had been real easy. But it was becoming more difficult. He had to make five hundred on this horse to repay two weeks' rent he had borrowed from the safe. When he got the job, the agent lectured him about keeping the accounts of the apartment building up-to-date and told him twice, "Keep the rent money safe in the office safe!" He had lost at the track and at the poker table all last week. And the Thunderbird. . . The 1-horse was the longest shot. If it came in, he would turn his fifty into five hundred, or five thousand. . .or five million, tax-free, as Bob liked to say. He felt safer betting with the Jamaican than with Bob. And he's a poker player too! Between this race and the poker game. . .lemme see, I should get back an even. . .

Bob was talking to him. "Let's watch this race and get some thrills for our money."

They went into the stands outside but every seat was taken. The space on the lawn in front of the stands was packed. "You were great last Sattadee night at the game. Shit, you hid that Ace in the hole and had everybody thinking you had only Ace-high. . . You musta pulled in four, five hundred bucks in that one pot. . ."

The horses were emerging from the tunnel. He looked at the 1-horse. A black groom was leading it. The groom looked into the stand in Pat's direction, recognized some- one, and Pat saw him wink and heard him say, "Cahn' lose!" And Pat began to replace all the rent money he had borrowed. He stopped watching the horses. He looked at the people, and he loved the world. In his mind he did all the chores: cleaned the driveway, repaired an old lady's stove, fixed a young couple's fuse box and washed the elevators. . .

Those goddamn immigrants always pissing in the elevators! When he was a tenant he could look at all this filth and look away, even though he always grumbled about it. But now that he was the super, each speck of filth meant hours of hard work. If I was still with Transportation, I would flunk every one of them!

His eyes passed like a camera panning over the vast crowd murmuring with excitement before the race. His eyes rested on a woman. She was beautiful in a sensual way. Her hair was dyed blonde. Even from the back she looked sexy. She was well-dressed. The crowd was hushed. He looked at the starting gate and saw his horse. It had danced before him as it paraded in front of the people. Something wrenched his eyes from the horse back over the multitude of people to the woman. His heart stopped beating. He recognized her. "Look at that bitch!" It was his wife. Beside her was the well-dressed Jamaican who, like him, had backed the same horse. In all the years I knew that broad, she never even read the goddamn sports pages! And look at that bitch now! If I was still with Transportation, I would flunk every goddamn. . .

Minutes later, after the 1-horse had come in third and Bob was laughing and dancing and talking about screwing Bahamian women, Pat was trying to roll his ticket into a small ball and fire it and shoot his wife, the bitch! The first time he had seen her at the track, and he had lost! Now he saw her leap into the air when the tote board gave the results. The Jamaican was smiling. He saw him hand her the ticket, and she climbed the steps to the cashiers' wickets. He pushed through the crowd to cut her off. "Get outta my goddamn way, nigger!"

A black man was moving too slowly for him.

"Hey!" someone yelled. But he was losing patience. "Watch it, buster!" he told the man.

"No, you watch it, fellow!" The voice that spoke was a Scottish brogue, a rich brogue of rebuke. "I say!" But he was losing his wife in the crowd to a Jamaican, and he didn't give a damn about Scottish ancestry now. He was losing his temper too.

"Rass, man! To-rass!"

He lost his temper. She stopped. He turned around. In front of him was a man much like the Jamaican with the red, black and green woollen cap. Men like you didn't talk back to me when I was with Transportation. I had men like you in my hand, in my power... He thought of his wife in bed with the Jamaican.

"You sonofa*bitch*!"

"Rass, mahn! What you call I?"

"You heard me!"

The Jamaican rushed at him. A crowd gathered. Bob saw him and pulled him from the Jamaican. Silently the crowd witnessed their exchange of violence with words. And when it was finished, when the words stopped and left only the bad smell of feeling, the crowd surged to the large glass wall to see the horses entered in the next race.

Bob patted him on his shoulder to quell the spirit in him. Then he started to check his winnings, holding the twenty-dollar bills spread like a fan, like playing cards. "That poker game *tonight*! The Jamaican fellow's coming. I know he walks with more money than a bank." Bob pushed his money into his pocket. "What did I tell ya? Didn't I give ya the 5-horse? Didn't I give ya a big winner? Didn't I pick 'em for ya?"

Tenants came and dropped their rent cheques through the slot in the door. The office was closed. He watched them fall. He was cleaning his own apartment for the poker game, so he ignored them, just as he had earlier ignored the leaves he walked over up at Woodbine, leaves like the tickets of wrong bets discarded on the vast cement floor of the clubhouse. The trees at Woodbine were like gold at this time of year. He liked to drag his feet through their fallen colours of gold and russet. Someone was pressing his buzzer.

These goddamn tenants! Don't they think I have a life of my own? I'm tired cleaning up after them. . . A fat black woman past middle age stood facing him. He tried to imagine what she looked like naked. She was smiling. He became sorry for his thoughts.

"Mr. Pat, boy, I bring your rent since the office closed." She came inside and sat down. "Lemme rest this weary body, boy. Work killing me. I don't know what keeping me in this cold place. Jamaica more better." She threw a cough drop into her mouth. "How you making out at the track? I hear you goes there every day."

"Canada's better than many places I know," he said. "Take the States, for instance."

"Me, child? There?. . .I paying you one month in advance. Count it. Five hundred, eh?" He had ignored her comment about the races. Now he watched her as a smile came over her face. He thought he saw a sparkle in her eyes. "In all the time I living here, you's the most decent super ever put in charge o' this building. I would hate to see you leave." What was she telling him? "The place looking the most decentest it ever look!"

He smiled and shook her hand after giving her the receipt. Absent-mindedly he put the five hundred dollars in his pocket. He watched her walk slowly along the shining corridor, and then she started sneezing and had to hold onto the wall for support. He had just sprayed the corridor with Lysol. She looked back and waved at him. "Have a good night. . ." And he stood at the door and watched her slowly become smaller.

* * *

42

He was happy and warm and fresh and clean. The shower did him good. His mind was clear and deadly. They had been playing poker for many hours now, and he was still concentrating. The six of them, including the well-dressed Jamaican, were still around the aluminium table on which he had spread a white bed sheet. He looked at the clock beneath his Canadian flag, and the hands showed him it was long after midnight. "Let's send out for some Kentucky fried," he said.

"I could eat a horse, to-rass!" the Jamaican said. "And Bob here could buy chicken for the whole building, the way he been kicking ass tonight."

"Chicken? Shit! First thing tomorrow, Sattadee, I purchasing my ticket to the Bahamas. I'm through with you bastards."

"That 5-horse ran like a motherfucker, eh, Bob?"

"They should shoot that 1-horse," Pat said. They all laughed. "Well, I'll call for the Kentucky fried."

And he went into his bedroom where the phone was. He was happy. He poured a little of his scotch on the ugly stubby plant. He may even pay for the whole order. He sat on a pillow. He eased the pillow from under him the moment he sat down, and when he moved it aside he realized he had placed his gun there. He gave the order and the address. He got up and left the gun exposed on the bed. He poured some more scotch on the stubby plant, and as he did it he cursed his wife; and he watered the stubby plant each time he thought of her. The plant was sturdier than he had thought. "In twenty minutes, gang," he announced when he rejoined them.

"Well, let's *deal*," the Jamaican said.

Bob started to sing "Brown Skin Gal." The Jamaican joined him. Bob changed to "Rum and Coca Cola."

"Let's make this the last game," he said.

"Let's make it a big one!" the Jamaican said. "To-rass. It's only bread."

Pat won the next three games. He was now completely out of debt. He could replace every outstanding rent payment he had borrowed. All of a sudden the Jamaican and he were the only two players left. The game was five card stud. The second cards were dealt. He had a King in the hole, and an Ace showing. Another King dropped in front of him. A four to the Jamaican. He could hear the others breathing hard. He bet twenty dollars as a bluff. The Jamaican looked at the pair of fours that had just dropped in front of him, peeped at his hole card, smiled and said, "Let's have some fun. 'Ere tonight, gone to-rass tomorrow, bredder!" He stared at Pat. "See your twenty, and raise you *one hundred* and twenty bucks, bredder!" The breathing stopped.

"Good night, Irene," he began to whistle through his teeth. It was a rasping, annoying sound. "Shit, I took a shot."

The next card Pat got was a four. This bastard's four! He was silently ecstatic. It's the last game anyhow.

The Jamaican started to count out two thousand dollars. He dropped the pile on the table. Pat felt that if he could win this pot, he would not only replace all the rent money but would also buy the Thunderbird.

"How much bread you have in this place, bredder?"

Pat looked at the clock. He looked at the Canadian flag, focusing on the large Maple Leaf, red and sturdy like his Scottish ancestry. He refused to answer the Jamaican. The Jamaican repeated the question, this time with some venom in his voice. I'm not your goddamn brother.

"Fifty," the Jamaican called, dragging out his bet as he looked Pat full in the eyes, "and five hundred. . . Five hundred and fifty, bredder."

Pat had three hundred dollars in front of him. But he remembered the five hundred in his pocket from the kind black lady. He had another thirteen hundred inside, in a drawer where he kept the cash from the rent money when the office was closed. He kept it there near his gun until the agent came to collect it.

"Are you calling, bredder?"

All Pat could hear was the hoarseness in the man's voice. He felt a tug at his guts. The others started to breathe again, harder. And they were standing up. Then it became very quiet. Pat could hear the clock ticking. "I have *nine* hundred and fifty," he said. "I raise!" His voice dropped a decibel.

The Jamaican jumped up. His eyes were red. He stared at his cards. He stared at Pat's cards. He seemed to be looking right through the cards to their turned-down faces. He was trying to remember something. He became tense. But there was anger in him too. He was concentrating on two cards which Pat had been dealt, trying to remember how he had bet when he got those cards. All of a sudden he broke wind. It was a loud, sharp, short blast.

"'Scuse me, bredder."

"You pass, or you fold, sonofa*bitch*?"

"Hell, no! I raise, man."

Pat could feel his feet dragging in leaves, and he could feel his guts in knots, and the fatigue of the long night brought a film to his eyes. He became cold. He got up and went into the bedroom. They heard a tap running. He came back, and without a word he counted two thousand dollars. He threw the bills on the table. They were like leaves. He imagined his fingers walking through them, gathering them all in.

I'm gonna take a trip myself. . .better still, put a down payment on a goddamn house, if that's what she wants. . . He could see her in the long sleek silk zebra nightgown. He saw the Jamaican touching her and the zebra cloth. *But she's mine, sonofabitch!* His hands began to shake. He put them on his thighs under the table, while Bob checked the pot to see if it was correct. Bob was smiling. The Jamaican was smiling. Pat's hands were moving up and down his thighs. His right hand touched something hard. Jesus Christ, am I getting hard? He was surprised at the hardness. But he felt warm again. Sure, I'm gonna buy the goddamn house for the kid, even if she's fucking around. . .

"Bob, did ya know my wife's going around with this son-ofa*bitch*?"

"Declare!" the Jamaican said when he called the bet.

The air remained tense. Pat looked at Bob and then into the Jamaican's eyes, and slowly he turned over his hole card. "Kings and Aces!" he shouted.

He was laughing with the flag. It wasn't the flag of a king, but what the hell! It was his flag. All his debts were paid.

"Acesandkings!" And his hands moved to the Maple Leafs of bills on the aluminium table. He felt it had been a duel. Over his wife. And he had won.

"Just one motherfucking minute, bredder!" The Jamaican held the long fingernail on his left hand's little finger and eased it under his own hole card. The air was stifling. And when the card was face upwards and Pat saw the three fours exposed and heard the applause and the noise, and Bob assuring and cursing him because, "Pat, didn't ya god-damn see that the goddamn *fourth* four wasn't exposed, even though you had one, and didn't ya remember that the two other Kings was folded in the goddamn pack, in the dead pack, and didn't ya notice that two other Aces was folded in the dead pack, didn't ya notice that, ya stupid bastard?"

Pat saw the Jamaican raking in the bills like leaves at this time of year, as the boys at the track at Woodbine collected discarded tickets, and he could hear the agent's voice on the telephone first thing tomorrow; and he thought he heard even more immediately the voice at the door saying over and over, "Taxi!"; and then all the noise of chairs falling and people running out of his apartment, and the raking of the leaves on the table; and how in a split second the room became quiet, and then moved like jello in his vision, and the Canadian flag which was the only thing he could focus on, and the empty soiled bed sheet. He did not even know when he got up from the table and moved towards the bedroom. . .

Griff!

GRIFF WAS A BLACK MAN FROM BARBADOS WHO sometimes denied he was black. Among black Americans who visited Toronto, he was black: "Right on!" "Peace and love, Brother!" and "Power to the people!" would suddenly become his vocabulary. He had emigrated to Toronto from Britain and, as a result, thought of himself as a black Englishman. But he was blacker than most West Indian immigrants. In colour, that is. It must have been this double indemnity of being British and black that caused him to despise his blackness. To his friends and his so-called friends he flaunted his British experience and the "civilized" bearing that came with it; and he liked being referred to as a West Indian who had lived in London, for he was convinced that he had an edge, in breeding, over those West Indians who had come straight to Canada from the cane-fields in the islands. He had attended Ascot many times and he had seen the Queen in her box. He hated to be regarded as just black.

"Griff, but you're blasted black, man," Clynn said once at a party in his own home, "and the sooner you realize that fact, the more rass-hole wiser you would be!" Clynn wasn't usually so honest, but that night he was drunk.

What bothered Griff along with his blackness was that

49

most of his friends were "getting through": cars and houses and "swinging parties" every Friday night, and a yearly trip back home for Christmas and for Carnival. Griff didn't have a cent in the bank. "And you don't even have *one* blasted child neither!" Clynn told him that same night.

But Griff was the best-dressed man present. They all envied him for that. And nobody but his wife knew how really poor he was in pocket. Griff smiled at them from behind his dark-green glasses. His wife smiled too, covering her embarrassment for her husband. She never criticized him in public, by gesture or by attitude, and she said very little to him about his ways in their incensed apartment. Nevertheless, she carried many burdens of fear and failure for her husband's apparent ambitionless attitudes. England had wiped some British manners on her too. Deep down inside, Griff was saying to Clynn and the others, *god-blindyougodblindyou!*

"Griffy, dear, pour your wife a scotch, darling. I've decided to enjoy myself." She was breathing as her yoga teacher had taught her to do.

And Griffy said, *godblindyougodblindyou!* again to Clynn, poured his wife her drink, poured himself a larger scotch on the rocks, and vowed, *I am going to drink all your scotch tonight, boy!*

This was his only consolation. Clynn's words had become wounds. Griff grew so centred around his own problems that he did not for one moment consider any emotional support coming from his wife. "She's just a nice kid," he told Clynn once behind her back. He had draped his wife in an aura of sanctity; and he would become angry to the point of violence when he thought his friends' conversation touched the aura in which he had clothed her: like taking her out on Friday and Saturday nights to the Cancer Calypso Club in the entrails of the city, where pimps and doctors and lonely immigrants hustled women and brushed reputations in a brotherhood of illegal liquor. And if the club got too crowded, Griff would feign a headache and somehow make his wife feel the throbbing pain of his migraine and take her home in a taxi. He would recover miraculously on his way back along Sherbourne Street, and with the tact of a good barrister-at-law, would make tracks back to the Cancer and dance the rest of the limp-shirt night with a woman below his social status, picked from amongst the lonely West Indian stags: his jacket let loose to the sweat and the freedom, his body sweet with the music, rejoicing in the happy absence of his wife in the sweeter presence of this woman.

But after these hiatuses of dance, free as the perspiration pouring down his face, his wife would be put to bed around midnight, high up in the elevator, high off the invisible hog of credit, high up on the American Express card and the Chargex card, and Griff would be tense for days. It was a tenseness which almost gripped him in a paralysis, as it almost strangled all the blood in his body when the time approached for payments of loans for furniture and the television and for debts, and these times always coincided with the approach of his paycheque, already earmarked against its exact value. In times of this kind of stress, like his anxiety at the racetrack when the performance of a horse contradicted his knowledge of horses and of the *Racing Form* and left him broke, he would grumble, "Money is *naught* all."

Losing his money would cause him to ride on streetcars, and he hated any kind of public transportation. He seemed to realize his blackness more intensely on public transportation: white people looking at him hard, questioning his presence, it seemed. It might be nothing more than the way his colour changed colour, going through a kaleidoscope of tints and shades under the varying lights of the streetcar. But Griff never saw it that way. To him, it was staring. And his British breeding told him that to look at a person you didn't know (except if she was a woman) was *infra dig*. *Infra dig* was the term he chose when he told Clynn about these incidents of people staring at him on the streetcars. The term would form itself on his wide thin lips, and he could never get the courage to spit it at the white people staring at him.

When he lost his money at the track, his wife, after not having had dinner or the money to buy food, would smile that half-censuring smile, a smile that told you she had been forced against the truth of her circumstances to believe that money was "naught all, at-all."

But left to herself, left to the ramblings of her mind and her aspirations and her fingers over the new broadloom in her girl-friend's home, where her hand clutched the tight sweating crystal glass of scotch on the rocks, her scotch seeming to absorb her unhappiness with the testimony of her friend's broadloom; or in Clynn's recreation room, which she called a "den"; in her new sponge of happiness, fabricated like the house in her dreams, she would put her smile around her husband's losses, and in the embrace they would both feel higher than anybody present because, "Griffy, dear, you were the only one there with a Masters of Arts."

"I have more brains than *all o' them* put together. They only coming on strong. But I don't have to come on strong, uh mean, I don't *have* to come on strong. . ."

One day at Greenwood racetrack Griff put his hand into his pocket and pulled out five twenty-dollar bills and put them on one horse: he put three of the five twenty-dollar bills on Number Six, *on the fucking nose — to win! So what?* (he had been drinking earlier in the Pilot Tavern), and he put the other two twenty-dollar bills on Number Six, *to show*. He had studied the *Racing Form* like a man studying torts: he would put it into his pocket, take it out again, read it in the bathroom as he trimmed his moustache; he then studied it on the sweet-smelling toilet bowl, he studied it as he might have studied laws in Britain; and when he spoke of his knowledge of thoroughbreds' history in the *Racing Form*, it was as if he had received his degrees in the laws of averages and not in English literature and language.

And he "gave" a horse to a stranger that same day at Greenwood. "Take the Number Three, man. I read the *Form* for three days, mekking notes. It *can't* lose!" The man thanked him because he himself was no expert; and he spent five dollars (more than he had ever bet before) on Number Three, *to win*. "I can read the *Form* like a blasted book, man!" Griff told the stranger. He then slipped from the stranger to the wicket farthest away; and like a thief, he bought his own tickets: "Gimme the Six-horse! Sixty on the nose! Forty to show!" and to himself he said, smiling, "Law o' averages, man. Law of averages!"

Tearing up the ticket on Number Six after the race, he said to the stranger who had looked for him to thank him, and who thanked him and shook his hand and smiled with him, "I don't have to come on strong, man. I *mastered that Form*! I can pick 'em!" He looked across the field at the tote board and checked the price paid on Number Three, and then he said to the stranger, "Lend me two dollars for the next race, man. I need a bet."

The stranger gave him three twenty-dollar bills and told him, "*Any* time, brethren, any time! Keep the sixty bucks. Thank *you*, sah!" The horse had won, going away, at sixty-to-one.

Griff left broke. Money is *naught* all, he was telling the same man who, seeing him waiting by the streetcar stop, had picked him up. Griff settled himself back in the soft red leather of the new black Riviera going west and said again to the man, no stranger now, "Money is naught all!

But I don't like to come on strong. Uh mean, you *see* how I picked 'em, didn't you?"

"To-rass, brethren! You right, to-rass!" the man said, adjusting the tone and the volume of the tape deck. "How you like my new wheels?"

The elevator was silent that evening on the way up to the twenty-fifth floor, and he could not even lose his temper with it. But two young women in the elevator with him started to giggle, and he thought, This country is uncivilized, even the elevators — they make too much noise, a man can't even think in them, this place only has money but it don't have any culture or breeding or class so everybody is grabbing for money money money.

The elevator that evening didn't make a comment. And neither did his wife. She had been waiting for him to come home from work, straight, with the money untouched in his monthly paycheque. But Griff had studied the *Racing Form* thoroughly all week and had worked out the laws of averages and notations in red ink. He circled all the "long shots" in green, and had moved through the "donkeys," the slow horses, with waves of blue lines. He had three "sure things" for that day, and had averaged his total winnings with the heavy bets from his monthly salary, it was such a sure thing, a "goddamn cinch"!

He had developed a migraine headache immediately after lunch, slipped through the emergency exit at the side, holding his head in his hand, his head also full of tips and cinches, and had caught the taxi which miraculously had been waiting there, with the meter ticking; had run through the entrance of the racetrack, up the stairs, straight for the wicket to bet on the Daily Double; had invested one hundred dollars on a "long shot" worked out scientifically on his red-marked, green-and-blue wavy-lined *Form*, and had placed "two goddamn dollars" on the favourite — just to be sure and for the fun of it — and went into the clubhouse. The favourite won. Griff had lost one hundred dollars by the end of the first race. But he had won two dollars on the favourite on his two-dollar bet.

"I didn't want to come on strong," he had told the stranger who was really a stranger then. The man could not understand what he was saying, and he asked for no explanation. "I didn't want to come on strong, but I worked out all the winners for today, since ten o'clock last night. I *picked* them, man. I can pick 'em. But I was going for the long shot. Hell, what is a little bread? One hundred dollars? Man, that isn't no bread at all. If I put my hand in my pocket now, look. . .*this* is bread!. . . Eight hundred dollars. I can lose, man. I can afford to lose in order to win. Money don't mean anything to me, man. Money is no *big* thing. Money is *naught* all."

His wife remained sitting on the Scandinavian couch which had the habit of whispering to them once a month, "Fifty-nine thirty-five owing on me, yuh!" She looked up at Griff as he gruffed through the door. She smiled. Griff grew stiff at the smile. She got up from the couch. She brushed the anxiety of time from her mini-skirt. ("My wife must dress well and look *sharp*, even in the house!") She tidied the already-tidy hairdo she had just got from Azans and went into the kitchen, which was now a wall separating Griff from her.

Griff looked at the furniture and wished he could sell it in time for the races tomorrow afternoon: the new unpaid-for living-room couch, desk, matching executive chair, the table and matching chairs where they ate, desk pens thrown into the bargain the salesman swore he was giving them ten Friday nights ago down Yonge Street, and scatter rugs, like Denmark in the fall season.

He looked at the motto, *Christ is the head of this home*, which his wife had insisted upon taking as another "bargain"; and he thought of how relaxed he felt driving in the man's new Riviera. He took the new *Racing Form*, folded in half and already notated, from his breast pocket and sat on the edge of the bed in the wisteria-smelling bedroom. The wife has been working, he said to himself, as he noticed he was sitting on his clean folded pyjamas. But he left them there and perused the handicaps and histories of the horses. The bundle buggy for shopping was rolling over the polished wood of the living-room floor. The hinges on the doors of the clothes cupboard in the hallway were talking. A clothes hanger dropped on the skating rink of the floor. The cupboard door was closed. The bundle buggy rolled down from its prop against the cupboard and jangled onto the hardboard ice. Griff looked up and saw a smooth brown, black-maned horse standing before him. It was his wife.

"Griffy, dear? I am ready." She had cleaned out her pocketbook of old papers, useless personal and business calling cards accumulated over drinks and at parties; and she had made a budget of her month's allowance and expenditures, leaving a place in the tidied wallet section for her husband's arrival. The horse in Griff's mind changed into a donkey.

"Clynn called. He's having a party tonight. Tenish. After the supermarket, I want to go around the corner to the cleaner's and stop off at the liquor store for a bottle of wine. My sisters're coming over for dinner, and they're bringing their boyfriends. I want to serve a roast. Should I also buy a bottle of Black-and-White scotch, Griffy, dear?" *They're at post! They're off. . .as they come into the back stretch, moving for the wire. . .it's Phil Kingston by two lengths, Crimson Admiral, third, True Willie. . .Phil Kingston, Crimson Admiral, True Willie. . .* But Griff had already moved downstairs in the direction of the cashiers' wicket: "Long shot in your arse! Uh got it this time, old man!" *True Willie is making a move. True Willie. . .Phil*

Kingston now by one length, True Willie is coming on on the outside! True Willie! It's True Willie!

"It's almost time for the supermarket to close, Griff, dear, and I won't like to be running around like a race horse, sweating and perspiring. I planned my housework and I tried to finish all my chores on time so I'll be fresh for when you came home. I took my time too doing my housework and I took a shower so I won't get excited by the time my sisters come and I didn't bother to go to my yoga class. . ." *It's True Willie by a neck! True Willie! What a run, ladies and gentlemen. What a run! True Willie's the winner, and now it's official!*

"And I even made a promise to budget this month so we'll save some money for all these bills we have to pay. We have to pay these bills and we never seem to be paying them off and the rent's due in two days, no, *today!* Oh, I forgot to tell you that the bank manager called about your loan, to say that. . ." *It's True Willie by a neck!*

Griff smashed all the furniture in the apartment in his mind, then walked through the door. "Oh, Griffy, dear, Stooly called to say he's getting a lift to the races tomorrow and if you're going, he wants you to. . ."

Griff was standing in the midst of a group of middle-class West Indians, all of whom pretended through the amount of liquor they drank and the "gashes they lashed" that they were still young black studs.

"Man, when I entered the door, she knew more better than to open her fucking mouth to me! To *me? Me?*" The listening red eyes understood the unspoken chastisement in his threatening voice. "Godblindyou! She knew better than *that.* Me? If she'd only opened her fucking mouth, I would have. . ." They raised their glasses, all of them, to their mouths, not exactly at the same time but sufficiently together to make it a ritualistic and harmonious approval among men.

"As man!" Griff said, then wet his lips. They would, each of them, have chastised their women in precisely the same way that Griff was boasting about disciplining his. But he never did. He could never even put his hand to his wife's mouth to stop her from talking. And she was not the kind of woman you would want to beat: she was much too delicate and sophisticated.

The history of their marriage had coincided with her history of a woman's illness which had been kept silent between them; and its physical manifestation, in the form of a large scar that crawled halfway around her neck, darker in colour than the natural shade of her skin, had always, from the day of recovery after the operation, been covered by a neckline on each of her dresses. And this became her natural style and fashion in clothes. Sometimes, in more daring moods, she would wear a silk scarf to hide the scar.

He bragged to Clynn one night. "If my wife wasn't so blasted sickly, I would put my hand in her arse *many times*! Many times I've thought o' putting my hand in her arse after a bad day at the races!" He had even thought of doing something more drastic about her supercilious smile and his losses at the track and at poker. It was not clearly shaped in his mind; and at times, with this violent intent, he could not think of whom he would perform this drastic act on. After a bad day at the track, the thought of the drastic act would beat him down and take its toll on his slim body which refused to bend under the psychological pressure of losing all the time.

He had just lost five hundred dollars at the larger track, Woodbine, and had entered Clynn's living room that evening for the usual Friday-night party of scotch and rum and West Indian peas and rice and chicken, which Clynn's Polish wife cooked and spoiled. He had just had time to adjust his shoulders in the oversized sports jacket when he said, as if bragging, "I just dropped *five*. At Woodbine." He wet his lips and smiled.

"Hundred?" Clynn asked.

"*No* big thing!" he said. "I've lost more at Greenwood."

"Dollars?" Clynn's powerful voice came from the dark corner of the "den" where he was pouring drinks. Clynn was a man who wouldn't lend his sister or his mother — if she was still alive — more than five dollars at one time.

"Money is *naught* all."

"You're a blasted. . . Boy, do you lose *just* for fun, or wha'?" Clynn sputtered. "Why the arse you don't become a *groom* if you like racehorse summuch? Or you's a. . .a. . . a *paffological* loser?"

"Uh mean, I don't like to come on strong or anything, but money is naught all. . ."

"Rass-hole, put down *my* scotch then! You drinking my scotch! And scotch cost money like shite!"

And it rested there. It rested there because Griff suddenly remembered he was among men who knew him; who knew his losses both in Britain and in Canada. It rested there also because Clynn and the others knew that his manner and attitude towards money, and his wife's expressionless smile, were perhaps lying expressions of a turbulent inner feeling of failure.

"He prob'ly got rass-hole ulcers too," Clynn said, and then spluttered into a laugh.

Griff thought about it and wondered whether he had indeed caused his wife to be changed into a different woman altogether. But he couldn't know that. Her smile covered a granite of silence. He wondered whether he hated her to the bone, and whether she hated him. He felt a spasm through his body as he thought of her hating him, and not knowing about it. For so many years living together, both here and in Britain; and she was always smiling. Her constancy and her cool exterior, her smiles, all made him wonder now, with the scotch in his hand, about her undying devotion to him, her faithfulness, pure as the sheets in their sweet-smelling bedroom. He wondered:

Should I throw my hand in her arse *just* to keep her honest?

But Clynn had made up his own mind that she was completely destroyed inside: her guts, her spirit, her aspirations, her procreative mechanism. "Hysterectomy all shot to shit!" Clynn said cruelly, destroyed beyond repair, beneath the silent consolation and support which he saw her giving to her husband, at home among friends and relations, and in public among his sometimes silently criticizing friends. "I don't mean to come on strong, but. . ."

"You really want to know what's wrong with Griff?" Clynn's sister, Princess, asked one day. "He want a *stiff* lash in his backside! He don't know that he gambling 'way his wife's life? He don't know that? Look, he don't have chick nor child. Wife working in a good job, for *decent* money, and they don't even live in a decent apartment that yuh could say, well, after all, um is the rent money that eating out his sal'ry. Don't even own a record player. *Nothing.* And all he doing is walking 'bout Toronto with his blasted head up in the air. He don't know this is North-amurca? Be-Christ, and he don't even want to speak to black people. He don't have no mottocar, like some. Well, you tell me then, what the bloody hell is Griff doing with nineteen thousand Canadian dollars a year? Supporting racehorse? No, man! You can't tell me that 'cause not even the most wutless o' Wessindians living in Toronto could gamble 'way nineteen thousand dollars! Jesus Christ, that is thirty-eight thousand back home in Barbados! Think o' the land he could buy back home wid nineteen thousand Canadian dollars. And spenning it 'pon a racehorse? What the hell is a racehorse? *Nineteen thousand?* But lissen to me. One o' these mornings that wife o' his going get up and tell he that she with child, that she *pregnant*. . ." ("She can't get pregnant, though, Princess, 'cause she already had one o' them operations!") "Anyhow, if his wife was a different person, she would have walk out on his arse *long ago*! Or else cut his blasted throat. And she won't spend a day in the Don Jail!"

When Griff heard what Princess had said about him, he shrugged his shoulders. "I don't have to come on strong, but if I was a different man, I would really show these West Indian women something. . ." He ran his long black fingers over his slim tie, shrugged the grey sports jacket that was a size too large at the shoulders into shape and place, wet his lips twice and said, "Gimme another scotch, man." While Clynn fixed the scotch, he ran the thumb and index finger of his left hand down the razor edge of his dark-brown trouser seams. He inhaled and tucked his shirt and tie neatly beneath the middle button of his jacket. He took the scotch, which he liked to drink on the rocks. "I don't have to come on strong, but I'm going to tell you something. . ."

The next Friday night was the first day of fete in the long weekend. There hadn't been a long weekend in Canada for some time. Everybody was tired of just going to work, coming home, watching CBC television, bad movies on TV, then going to bed.

"There ain' no action in this fucking town," Clynn was saying for days before the weekend appeared like raindrops on a farmer's dry-season head. And everybody agreed with him. It was so. Friday night was here, and the boys, their wives, their girl friends and their "outside women" were noisy and drunk and happy. Some of the men were showing off their new bell-bottom trousers and broad leather belts worn under their bulging bellies to make them look younger.

The women, their heads shining like wet West Indian tar roads, the smell from the cosmetics and grease that went into their kinky hair and on their faces to make them look sleek and smooth, all these smells mixed with the cheap domestic perfumes they used. And some women, wives whose husbands "were getting through," were wearing good-looking dresses in style. Others were still back home in their style, poured into dresses against their wishes and the better judgement of their bulging bodies; backsides big, sometimes too big, breasts bigger, waists fading into the turbulence of their middle age, and their behinds, all poured against the shape of their noisy bodies, into evil-fitting shiny outfits made on a borrowed sewing machine on sleepy nights after work.

But everybody was happy. They had all forgotten now, through the flavour of the calypso and the peas and rice, the fried chicken, the curry goat, that they were still living in a white man's country; and it didn't seem to bother them now. Tonight none of them would tell you that they hated Canada; that they wanted to go back home; that they were going to "make a little money first"; that they were only waiting till then, that they were going to go back before the blasted Canadian "tourisses buy up the blasted Carbean." They wouldn't tell you tonight that they all suffered some form of racial discrimination in Canada and that it was to be expected since "there are certain things with this place that are not just right." Not tonight. Tonight, Friday night, was forgetting night. West Indian night. And they were at the Cancer Club to forget and to drink and get drunk. To make plans for some strange woman's (or man's) body and bed, to spend "some time" with a real West Indian "thing," to eat her boiled mackerel and green bananas, which their wives and women had, in their ambitions to be "decent" and Canadian, for-gotten how to cook and left out of their diets, especially when Canadian friends were coming to dinner, because that kind of food was "plain Wessindian stupidness." Tonight they would forget and drink, forget and dance, and dance to forget.

"Oh, Jesus Christ, Griff!" Stooly shouted as if he was

singing a calypso. He greeted Griff this way each time he came to the Cancer; and each time it was as if Stooly hadn't seen Griff in months, although they might have been together at the track the same afternoon. It was just the way Stooly was. "Oh, Jesus Christ, Griff!" he would shout, and then he would rush past Griff, ignoring him, and make straight for Griff's wife. He would wrap his arms around her slender body (once his left hand squeezed a nipple, and Griff saw and said to himself, "Uh mean, I won't like to come on strong about it, but. . ." and did nothing about it). He'd pull her new mini-dress above the length of decency, worn for the first time tonight, exposing the expensive lace which bordered the tip of her slip. The veins of her hidden age, visible only at the back of her legs, would be exposed to Griff, who would stand and stare; and as the other man's hands inquired all over his wife's body, he would feel the blood and passion and love mix with the rum in his mouth. Sometimes, when in a passion of brandy, he would make love to his wife as if she was a different woman, as if she was no different from one of the lost women found after midnight on the crowded familiar floor of the Cancer.

"Haiiii! How?" the wife would say all the time her body was being crushed by Stooly. She would say "Haiiii! How?" every time it happened; and it happened every time; and every time it happened, Griff would stand and stare and do nothing about it because his memory of British breeding told him so; but he would feel mad and helpless afterwards, all night; and he would always want to kill Stooly or kill his wife for doing it. But he always felt she was so fragile. He would want to kill Stooly more than he would want to kill his wife. But Stooly had come from the same island as his wife.

Griff would tell Clynn the next day on the telephone that he should have done something about it; but he didn't "because he didn't want to come on strong." Apparently, he was not strong enough to rescue his wife from the rape of Stooly's arms as Stooly rubbed his body against hers like a dog scratching its fleas against a tree.

Once a complete stranger saw it happen. Griff had just ordered three drinks: one for his wife, one for himself and one for Stooly, his friend. Griff looked at the man and in an expansive mood (he had made the "long shot" in the last race at Woodbine that afternoon at fifty-to-one) he asked the stranger, "What're you drinking?"

"Rum, sah!"

"I am going to buy you a goddamn drink just because I like you, man."

The stranger did not change the mask on his face but stood there looking at Griff's dark-green glasses. Then he said, "You isn' no blasted man at all, sah!" He then looked behind: Stooly was still embracing Griff's wife. It looked as if he was feeling her up. The man took the drink from Griff and said, "You is no man, sah."

Griff laughed but no noise came out of his mouth. "Man, that's all right. They went to school together in Trinidad."

"In *my* books, you still ain' no fucking man, boy!" The stranger turned away from Griff, and when he got to the door of the dance floor, he said, "But thanks for the drink, *boy*."

The wife was standing beside Griff now, smiling as if she was a queen parading through admiring lines of subjects. She looked, as she smiled, like she was under the floodlights of some premiere performance she had prepared herself for a long time. She smiled, although no one in particular expected a smile from her. Her smiling went hand in hand with her new outfit. It had to be worn with a smile. It looked good on her, as usual, and it probably understood that it could only continue to look good and express her personality if she continued smiling. At intervals during

64

the night when you looked at her, it seemed as if she had taken the smile from her handbag and powdered it onto her face. She could have taken it off any time, but she chose to wear it the whole night.

"Griffy, dear?" she said, although she wasn't asking him anything or telling him anything or even looking in his direction. "Haiiii! How?" she said to a man who brushed against her hips as he passed. The man looked frightened because he wanted his advance to remain stealthy and masculine. When he passed back with five glasses of cheap rum and cokes in his hands, he walked far from her.

Griff was now leaning on the bar, facing the part-time barman and talking about the results of the last race that day. His wife, her back to the bar, was looking at the men and women, and smiling. When someone passed who noticed her and lingered in recognition, she would say "Haiiii! How?"

A large, black, badly dressed Jamaican (he was talking his way through the crowd) passed. He stared at her. She smiled. He put out his calloused hand, hardened from construction work, and with a little effort he said, "May I have this dance, daughter?"

Griff was still talking, but in his mind he wondered whether his wife would dance with the Jamaican. He became ashamed of himself for thinking about it. He went back to talking and got into an argument with the part-time barman, Masher, over a certain horse that was running in the feature race the next day at Woodbine. Masher, ever watchful over the women, especially other men's, couldn't help notice that the Jamaican's calloused hand was holding Griff's wife's hand. With his shark eyes he tried to get Griff's attention off horses and onto his wife, but Griff was too preoccupied.

His wife placed her drink on the counter beside him, her left hand still in the paws of the Jamaican construction worker whom nobody had seen before, and she said, "Griffy, dear?"

The man's hand on her manicured fingers had just come into consciousness when Griff wheeled around to give her the drink. He was upset. But he tried to be cool. It was the blackness of the Jamaican. And his size. Masher knew he was upset. The Jamaican reminded Griff of the Congoman in one of Sparrow's calypsos. Masher started to laugh in his spitting kee-kee laugh. And when Griff saw that everybody was laughing and had seen the Jamaican Congoman walk off with his wife, he too decided to laugh.

"It's all right, man," he said more than twice to no one in particular, although he could have been consoling the Jamaican Congoman or Masher or the people nearby or himself.

"I sorry, sah," the Jamaican said. He smiled to show Griff that he was not a rough fellow. "I am sorry, sah. I didn't know you was with the missus. I thought the daughter was by sheself tonight again, sah."

"It's no big thing, man," Griff said, turning back to talk to Masher who by now had lost all interest in the horses. Masher had had his eyes on Griff's wife too. But Griff was worried by something new now: the man had said, *by sheself tonight again, sah*. And that could mean only one thing: that his wife went places, like this very club, when he wasn't with her. He had never thought of this, and never even imagined her doing a thing like this, and he wasn't sure that it was not merely the bad grammar of the Jamaican and not the accusation in that bad grammar.

"Never mind that the fellow looks like a cane-cutter, he's still a brother," Griff said to Masher, but he could have been talking to Clynn or even to himself. "I don't want to come on strong, but he's a brother." The CBC television news that night had dealt with black solidarity in the States.

The Jamaican and Griff's wife were now on the dance floor. Griff stole a glimpse at them to see if the man was holding his wife in the same friendly way as Stooly would hold her. He thought he would be able to find the meaning of *by sheself, again* and *tonight* in the way the man held her. Had the Jamaican done so, Griff would have had to think even more seriously about the four words. But the Jamaican was about two hundred and fifty pounds of muscle and mackerel and green bananas. "Some other fellow would have come on strong just because a rough-looking chap like him held on. . ."

"Man, Griff, you's a rass-hole idiot, man!" Masher said. He crept under the bar counter, came out, faced Griff, broke into a sneering laugh and said, "You's a rass-hole." Griff laughed too in his voiceless laugh. "You didn't hear that man say *by herself tonight again*? If I had a woman like that, I would beat her arse, be-Christ, just for *looking* at a man like that Jamaikianman!" Masher laughed some more and walked away, singing the calypso the amateur band was trying to play, *"Oh Mister Walker, Uh come to see your daughter. . ."*

Griff wet his lips. His bottom lip disappeared inside his mouth, under his top lip; then he did the same thing with his top lip. He adjusted his dark glasses and ran his right hand, with a cigarette in it, over his slim tie. His right hand was trembling. He shrugged his sports jacket into place and shape on his shoulders. . . *"Oh Mister Walker, Uh come to see ya daughterrrrr. . ."*

He stood by himself in the crowd of West Indians at the entrance, and he seemed to be alone on a sunsetting beach back in Barbados. Only the waves in the voice of the calypsonian, and the rumbling of the Congo drum, and the whispering, the loud whispering in the breakers of the people standing nearby, were with him. He was like the sea. He was like a man in the sea. He was a man at sea. . .

"tell she is the man from Sangre Grande. . ."

The dance floor was suddenly crowded, jam-packed. Hands were going up in the air, and some under dresses, in exuberance after the music. The words in the calypso were tickling some appetites. He thought of his wife's appetite and of the Jamaican's, who could no longer be seen in the gloom of the thick black crowd; and tomorrow was races, and he had again mastered the *Racing Form*. And Griff suddenly became terrified about his wife's safety and purity.

Out of the crowd he could see Masher's big red eyes and his teeth skinned in a mocking laugh. Masher was singing the words of the calypso: *"Tell she I come for she. . ."* The music and the waves on the beach, when the sun went behind the happy afternoon, rose like a gigantic sea, swelling and roaring as it came to where he was standing in the wet white sand; and the people beside him, whispering like birds going home to branches and rooftops, some whispering, some humming like the sea, fishing for fish and supper and for happiness, no longer in sight against the blackening dusk. . . *"She know me well, I had she already. . ."*

Stooly walked in front of him, like the lightning that jig-sawed over the rushing waves, and behind Stooly was a woman, a noisy Trinidadian, screaming, "This partee can't done till morning come!", like an empty can tied to a motorcar bumper. All of a sudden the fishermen were climbing out of their boats laden with catches, their legs wet up to their knees; and they walked with their boats up to the brink of the sand. In their hands were the fish.

Stooly still held the hand of the woman who was now walking and talking aloud, "Fete for so!" She was like a barracuda.

Masher and a woman he didn't know were walking like Siamese twins. One of his hands could not be seen. Out of the sea, now resting from the turbulent Congo drumming of the waves in the calypso, came the Jamaican Congoman and Griff's wife.

"Thank you very much, sah," he said, handing Griff his wife's hand. With the other, she was pulling her mini-skirt into place. "She is a first-class dancer, sah."

"Don't have to come on *strong*, man."

"If I may, some other time, I would like to. . ." the man said, smiling and wiping perspiration from his face with a red handkerchief. His voice was pleasant and it had an English accent hidden somewhere in it. But all the words Griff heard were *She know me well, I had she already. . . by sheself tonight again. . .* and there were races tomorrow.

His wife was smiling, smiling like the everlasting sea at calm. "Haiiii!" she said and smiled again.

The Jamaican moved back into the sea for more dancing and fish. The beach was still crowded; and in Griff's mind it was crowded, but there was no one but he standing among the broken forgotten pieces of fish: heads and tails and empty glasses and cigarette butts and some scales broken off in the bargain, or by chance, and the ripped-up tickets of wrong bets.

Masher appeared and said in his ear, "If she was my wife, be-Christ, I tell you. . ." and he left the rest for the imagination.

Griff's wife's voice continued, "Griffy, dear?"

Masher came back from the bar with a coke for the woman he was with. When he got close to Griff, he said in his ear, "Even if she was only just a screw, like that one I have there. . ."

"Griffy, dear? Let's go home, I am feeling. . ."

". . .and if you was *something*," Masher was now screaming down the stairs after them. Griff was thinking of the four little words which had brought such a great lump of weakness within the pit of his stomach.

"Masher seems quite happy tonight, eh, Griffy, dear? I never quite saw Masher so happy."

". . .you *boy*! You boy! *You*. . ."

"Masher, haiiii! How?"

"If it was mine," Masher shouted, trying to hide the meaning in his message, "if it was mine, and I had put only a two-dollar bet on that horse, that horse we was talking about, and that horse *behave* so, well, I would have to *lash* that horse till. . .*unnerstan*?"

"Griffy, dear? Masher really loves horses, doesn't he, eh?"

They were around the first corner, going down the last flight of stairs, holding the rails on the right-hand side. Griff realized that the stairs were smelling of stale urine, although he could not tell why. His wife put her arm around his waist. It was the first time for the day. "I had a great time, a real ball, a *lovely* time!"

Griff said nothing. He was tired. But he was also tense inside. Still, he didn't have the strength or the courage, whichever it was he needed, to tell her how he felt, how she had humiliated him, in that peculiar West Indian way of looking at small matters, in front of all those people. He could not tell her how he felt each time he watched Stooly put his arms around her slender body; and how he felt when the strange Jamaican man, with his cluttered use of grammar broken beyond meaning and comprehension, had destroyed something like a dream which he had had about her for all these fifteen years of marriage.

"Griffy, dear? Didn't you enjoy yourself?" Her voice was like a flower, tender and caressing. The calypso band had just started up again. And the quiet waltz seemed to have been chosen to make him look foolish. He could hear the scrambling of men and crabs trying to find dancing partners. He could imagine himself in the rush of fisher-men after catches. He was thinking of getting his wife

70

home quickly and coming back, to face Stooly and the Jamaican; and he wished that if he did come back they would both be gone, so he wouldn't have to come on strong. But he was thinking more of getting rid of his wife and coming back to dance and discuss the *Racing Form*; and tomorrow was races again.

He saw Stooly grabbing some woman's hand, a woman he had never seen before. But it was *his* club. He saw Masher, his eyes bulging and his mouth wide open, red and white, in joy. And Griff found himself not knowing what to do with his hands. He took them out of his jacket pockets. And his wife, examining her mini-dress in the reflection of the glass in the street door they were approaching, and where they always waited for the taxicab, removed her arm from his waist. Griff placed his hand on her shoulder near the scar, and she shuddered a little, and then he placed both hands on her shoulders. She straightened up, with the smile on her face, waiting for the kiss (he always kissed her like that), which would be fun, which was the only logical thing to do with his hands in that position around her neck, which would be fun and a little naughty for their ages, like the old times in Britain. And his wife, expecting this reminder of happier nights in unhappy London, relaxed, remembering both her doctor and her yoga teacher, and in the excitement of her usually unexcitable nature, was about to adjust her body to his and lean her scarred neck a little bit backward to make it easy for him, when she realized that Griff's hands had walked up from her shoulders and were now caressing the scar on her neck, hidden tonight by a paisley scarf. She shuddered in anticipation.

He thought of Stooly, as she thought of the Jamaican, as he thought of Masher, as he squeezed. . .tomorrow the first race goes at 1:45 p.m. And the more he squeezed, the less he thought of other things, and the less those things bothered him, and the less he thought of the flesh under his fingers, the scar which was becoming visible as his hands rumpled the neckline.

He was not quite sure what he was doing, what he wanted to do, for he was a man who always insisted that he didn't like to come on strong, and to be standing up here in a grubby hallway killing his wife would be coming on strong, and *infra dig*. He was not sure whether he was wrapping his hands around her neck in a passionate embrace imitating the Jamaican, or whether he was merely killing her.

But she was still smiling, the usual smile. He even expected her to say "Haiiii! How?" But she didn't. She couldn't. He didn't know where his kiss began and ended; and he didn't know when his hands stopped squeezing her neck. He looked back up the stairs, and he wanted so desperately to go back into the club and show them or talk to them, although he did not know exactly why, and what he would have done had he gone back into the club.

His wife's smile was still on her body. Her paisley scarf was falling down her bosom like a rich splatter of baby food, pumpkin and tomato sauce; and she was like a child, propped up against a wall, in anticipation of its first step, toddling into movement. But there was no movement. The smile was there, and that was all. He was on the beach again, and he was looking down at a fish, into the eye of reflected lead, a fish left by a fisherman on the beach. He thought he saw the scales moving up and down, like small bellows, but there was no movement. He had killed her. But he did not kill her smile. He wanted to kill her smile more than he wanted to kill his wife.

Griff wet his lips and walked back up the stairs. His wife was standing against the wall by the door, and she looked as if she was dead, and at the same time she looked as if she was living. It must have been the smile. As he reached the door, Griff thought he heard her whisper, "Griffy, dear?"

Stooly took away his arm from the strange woman's body and rushed to Griff, screaming as if he was bellowing out a calypso line, "Oh, Jesus Christ, Griff!"

Masher heard the name called and came laughing and shouting, "Jesus Christ, boy! You get rid o' the wife real quick, man! As man. *As man!*"

Griff was wetting his lips again. He shrugged his sports jacket into place and his mind wandered. "...show me the kiss-me-arse *Racing Form*, man. We going to the races tomorrow..."

Doing Right

I SEE HIM AND I WATCH HIM. I SEE HIM AND I WATCH him and I start to pray for him 'cause I see him heading for trouble. Making money. "In five or six years I want to have a lotta money. Only when I have a lotta dollars will people respect me." That is all Cleveland telling me.

I had to laugh. Every time he say so, I had to laugh 'cause I couldn't do nothing better than laugh.

"Look at the Rockefellers. Look at the Rothschilds. Look at the Kennedys."

I was going ask him if he know how they make their money. But before I could ask, he would be off dreaming and looking up at the ceiling where there was only cobwebs and dust. And only God knows what was circulating through his head every time he put himself in these deep reveries concerning making lots o' money and talking 'bout the Rockefellers, the Rothschilds and the Kennedys.

I was still laughing. 'Cause the present job he had was a green-hornet job. He was a man who went to work in a green suit from head to foot, except for the shoes which was black and which he never polish. His profession was to go round the St. Clair-Oakwood area putting parking tickets 'pon people cars. Before this, he uses to be on the Queens Park beat for green hornets.

A big man like him, over two hundred pounds, healthy and strong and black, and all he could do for eight or nine years is to walk 'bout with a little book in his hand, putting little yellow pieces o' paper on people windshields. He like the job so much and thought he doing the right thing that in the middle o' the night, during a poker game, or just dipsy-doodling and talking 'bout women, he would put back on the green uniform jacket, grabble up the peak cap, jump in the little green car that the police give him, and gone up by St. Clair-Oakwood, up and down Northcliffe Boulevard, swing right on Eglinton, gone down Eglinton, and swing left on Park Hill Road, left again on Whitmore, and all he doing is putting these yellow pieces o' paper on decent hard-working people cars. When he return, he does be laughing. I tell him he going soon stop laughing when a Wessindian lick he down with a big rock.

"I fix them! I have ticketed one hundred and ten motto-cars today alone! And the night I leff the poker game, I ticket fifty more bastards, mainly Wessindians."

I start to get real frighten. 'Cause I know a lotta these same Wessindians in them very streets where he does be ticketing and laughing. And all them Wessindians know who the green hornet is. And being as how they is Wessindians, I know they don't like green hornets, nor nobody who does be touching their cars. So I feel that any morning, when one o' these Wessindians come home from a party, or offa a night shift, and see him doing foolishness and putting yellow tickets on their motto-cars, I know um is at least *one* hand brek. Wessindians accustom to parking in the middle o' the road or on the wrong side back home. And nobody don't trouble them, nor touch their cars. And since they come here, many o' these Wessindians haven't change their attitude in regards to who own the public road and who own the motto-cars.

So whilst the boy still ticketing and laughing and putting

his hands on people cars which they just wash in the car wash on Bathurst, I continue worrying and watching him.

One night just as we sit down to cut the cards, and before the cards deal, he come in grinning and saying, "I ticket two hundred motto-cars today alone!"

"One-o' these days, boy!" I tell him.

"When I pass in the green car and I see him, I know I had him!"

"Who?"

"I see the car park by the fire hydrand. The chauffeur leaning back in the seat. One hand outside the car window. With a cigarette in tha' hand. The next hand over the back o' the seat. I look in the car, and when I look in, I nearly had a fit. I recognize the pipe. I recognize the dark-blue pin-stripe suit. I recognize the hair. With the streak o' grey in um. And I mek a U-turn in the middle o' the road. . ."

"But a U-turn illegal!"

"I is a green hornet, man!"

"I see."

"I size up the car. And I see the licents plate. ONT-001! I start getting nervous now. 'Cause I know it is the big man. Or the second big man in Toronto. I draw up. The chauffeur nod to me and tell me, "Fine day, eh?" I tell him, "A very fine day, sir!" And I get out. I bend over the bonnet o' this big shiny black car. . ."

"Limousine, man. A big car is call a limo."

"Well, um could have been a limo, a hearse or a automobile, I still bend over the bonnet and stick on one o' the prettiest parking tickets in my whole career!"

"The Premier's car?"

"He mek the law."

"And you think you do the right thing?"

"My legal duty. Afterwards, I did feel so good, like a real police officer, and not a mere green hornet. And I walk through Queens Park on my two feet, looking for more official cars to ticket. And when I was finish, I had stick on *five* parking tickets in their arse. One belongst to the Attorney-General, too."

"The same man who does defend Wessindians?"

"I put one 'pon Treasurer's car, too."

Well, that whole night, all the boy talking 'bout and laughing 'bout is how he stick on tickets on these big-shots' cars or limousines. And to make matters worse for the rest o' we, he win all the money in the poker game, too. I feel now that the boy really going become important, maybe become a real police, and make money. Or else going lose a hand or a foot.

But we was feeling good, though. 'Cause the big boys in Toronto don't notice we unless um is Caribana weekend, or when election time coming and they looking for votes, or when the *Star* doing a feature on Wessindians and racism and they want a quotation. Still, we feel this green hornet is our ambassador, even if he is only a ambassador o' parking tickets. So we laugh like hell at the boy's prowess and progress.

And we does wait till a certain time on a Friday night, nervous whilst cutting and dealing the cards, to see if the boy going turn up still dress off in the green uniform, meaning that he hasn't get fired for ticketing the big-shots' cars. And when he *does* turn up, dress from head to trousers in green, we know he still have the job and we does laugh some more. But all the time I still nervous as I seeing him and watching him.

Then he start lossing weight. He start biting his fingers. He start wearing the green uniform not press, and half dirty. He start calling we, "*You* people!"

I getting frighten 'cause he had just tell me that they tek him off the Queens Park beat for good.

So, um is now that he up in St. Clair-Oakwood, and I feel he going put a ticket on the *wrong* motto-car, meaning a Wessindian car. And at least one hand brek. Or one foot. And if the particular motto-car belongst to a Jamaican, not even the ones that have locks and does wear the wool tams make outta black, green and red, I know um could be *both* foots and *both* hands!

I see him and I watch him.

"I live in Trinidad, as a police. I leff Trinidad because they won't let me ticket one hundred more cars and break the all-time record. I went to Guyana after Trinidad. I was a police in Guyana before Guyana was Guyana, and was still Demerara or BG. They make me leff Guyana when I get close to the record. Ten more tickets is all I had to ticket. From Guyana, I end up in Dominica. Same thing. From Dominica, I went to Antigua, and um was in Antigua that a fellow came close to licking me down for doing my legal duty, namely ticketing cars. In all them countries, I ticket cars belonging to prime ministers, ministers of guvvament, priests, civil servants and school teachers."

I see him and I watch him. I see him getting more older than the forty-five years he say he was born. And I see him drinking straight white rums first thing every morning lately because he say, "The nerves bad. Not that I becoming a alcoholic, I only taking the bad taste o' waking up so early and the bitterness o' disappointment outta my mouth. I am not a alcoholic, though."

But he was drunk. Cleveland was drunk drunk drunk early every day. He had to be even more drunk after he outline his plan to make money.

"Remember the Rockefellers, man!" he tell me. "This is my plan. I been a green hornet for eight to nine years now. They promise me that if I ticket the most cars outta the whole group o' hornets they would send me to training school, to be a police. First they tell me I too short. I is five-four. But most criminals is five-three. Then they tell me that my arches fallen. Jesus Christ! What you expect?

After all the beats I walk in Trinidad, Guyana, Antigua, Dominica and Grenada, my arches bound to fall! And eight-nine years in this damn country pounding the beat ticketing cars! But they can't beat me. Not me. This is the plan I got for them. Tickets begin at five dollars. Right? There is five dollars, ten dollars and fifteen dollars. Twenty dollars for parking beside a fire hydrand, or on the wrong side. Now I write up a ten-dollar ticket. And I change the ten to a forty. The stub in my book saying ten. But the ticket on the car saying ten also, which I going change from ten to a forty. Then I rush down to the place on Wellesley Street where they have all them computers. And I tell the fellow I know from Guyana something, *anything,* to get him to look up the registration for me. And then I get in touch with the owner o' the car, and subtract ten from forty, and. . ."

"You mean subtract ten years from forty!"

"You don't like my plan?"

"I think your plan worth ten years."

"Okay. What about this one? People don't lock their cars when they park. Right? Wessindians is the biggest ones. Right? A fellow don't lock his car. And um is night. And I got on my green-hornet uniform. Right? Meaning I am still in a official capacity. . . ."

I see the boy start to smile and his face spread and look like a new moon. The face was shining, too, 'cause the heat and the sureness that the plan going work this time make him sweat real bad. But I watching him. I know that Wessindians don't have much money because they does get the worst and lowest-paying jobs in Toronto. Only a certain kind o' Wessindian does have money in their pocket. The kind that does work night shift, especially after midnight, when everybody else sleeping — the brand o' Wessindian who I not going mention by name *in case* they accuse me of categorizing the race. But *certain* Wessindians, like hairdressers, real estate salesmen and fellows who know racehorses good good good, *plus* the unmentionable afore-mentioned brand, and the illegal immigrants, the illegal parkers, and them who hiding from the police, all them so does have money to burn, inside their cars that not locked.

The boy eyes smiling. I see dollar bills instead o' pupils. I even hear the money clinking like when a car pass over the piece o' black rubber thing in a gas station. *Cling-cling*. "Gimme three months," he say. "Gimme three months, and I going show you something."

Just as I left him, and walking 'cross Northcliffe Boule-vard going to Eglinton, I see a green-hornet fellow standing up in front a man car. The man already inside the car. The man want to drive off. But the green-hornet fellow standing up in front the man car. The man inside the car honk the horn. And the green-hornet fellow take out his black book. Slow-slow. And he flip back a page. And hold down a little. And start to write down the car licents. The man honk the car again. The hornet walk more closer. He tear off the little yellow piece o' paper. And getting ready to put it on the man brand-new grey Thunderbird. Just as the hornet was about to ticket the man for parking next to a yellow fire hydrand, the fellow jump out. A Japanese sumo wrestler would have look like a twig beside o' him. Pure muscle. Shoes shining bright. White shirt. Stripe tie. Three-piece grey suit. Hair slick back. And long. Gold on two fingers on each hand. Gold on left wrist. More gold on right wrist. The hornet par'lyzed now. A rigor mortis of fear turn the whole uniform and the hornet inside it to starch, or like how a pair o' pyjamas does look when you left um out on the line in the dead o' winter.

"Goddamn!" the man say.

"You park wrong," the hornet say.

"Who say I park wrong?"

"You park illegal."

"Who goddamn say I park illegal?"

"Look at the sign."

"Which goddamn sign?"

"The sign say *no parking* between four and six. And *no stopping anytime*. You not only park, but you stop. You stationary, too." The Indian green-hornet man's voice get high and shaky.

"Ahmma gonna give you two seconds, nigger, to take that goddamn ticket off my car, motherfucker!"

"What you call me? I am not nigger. I am Indian. Legal immigrant. I just doing my job for the City of Toronto in Metropolitan Toronto. *You* are a blasted Amurcan Negro!"

All of a sudden I see how multiculturalism gone out the window now! I start seeing all them pamphlets and television commercials that show people of all colours like we laughing together and saying, "We is Canadians." All them advertisements in *Saturday Night* and *Maclean's,* and I remember how one minister up in Ottawa say different cultures have make up this great unified country of ours. I remember it word for word. All that lick up now.

The Goliath of a man grabble hold of the hornet by the scruff of the green uniform, the peak cap fall off all like now so, the little black book slide under the car, the hornet himself lifted offa the ground by at least three inches, and shaking 'bout in the gulliver's hands, pelting 'bout his two legs like if he is a muppet or a poppet. And when I think that the man going pelt the hornet fellow in the broad road, the man just hefted him up a little more higher offa the ground and lay him 'cross the bonnet of the shining Thunderbird, holding he down like how you does hold down a cat to tickle he under his chin. And the man say, "Now, motherfucker! Is you gonna take the goddamn ticket off my Bird?"

I pass quick, bo', 'cause I know the police does be up in this St. Clair-Oakwood district like flies round a crocus bag o' sugar, at the drop of a red, green and black cloth hat; and that they does tek in anybody who near the scene o' crime, no matter how small the scene or how small the crime. And if um is Wessindians, pure handcuffs and pelting 'bout inside the back o' cruisers till they get you inside the station. And then the real sport does start! So I looking and I looking off, knowing that a green hornet, even if he look like a Pakistani or a Indian but is really a Trinidadian or a Guyanese and only look a little Indian, going get help from the police. Not one police, but five carloads o' police.

All like now so, the road full up with Wessindians and other people, and these Wessindians looking on and laughing 'cause none o' them don't business with green hornets, not even green hornets that come from the Wessindies!

I pass 'long quick, bo'. I got to face the Immigration people in a week, and I don't want nothing concerning my past or present to be a stain through witnessing violence, to prevent them from stamping *landed immigrant* or *immigrant recu* in my Barbados passport! I may be a accessory before the fact. But I was still thinking of my friend, the other green hornet, so I look back to see what kind o' judgement the Thunderbird man was going to make with the Indian gentleman, who now have no peak cap, no black notebook, one shoe fall off and the green tunic tear up. And as my two eyes rested on the scene, *after the fact,* I hear the Charles Atlas of a man say, "And *don't* call the motherfucking cops! I got you covered, nigger. I knows where you goddamn live!"

I hope that this Goliath of a man don't know where my green-hornet friend does live! I hope the Thunderbird don't be park all the time up here! And I start to think 'bout getting a little message to my friend to tell him to don't put no tickets on no grey Thunderbirds or no Wessindian cars, like Tornados, whiching is Wessindians' favourite cars. And I start to wonder if he know that a

Wessindian does treat a Tornado more better than he does treat a woman or a wife. And with a Wessindian, yuh can't ask his woman for a dance at a dance, unless you expecting some blows. Even if he give you permission, don't dance a Isaac Hayes or a Barry White slow piece too slow and too close, yuh. . .

I waiting anxious now 'cause I don't see the boy for days these days. I feel the boy really making money from the scheme. I walk all over St. Clair-Oakwood, all along Northcliffe, swing right 'pon Eglinton, mek a left on Park Hill Road, a further left up by Whitmore and find myself back on Northcliffe going now in the opposite direction, and still I can't rest my two eyes on the green hornet. Fellows start telling me that the boy going to the races every day on his lunch break from ticketing people cars, and betting *one hundred dollars on the nose* and *five hundred to show* on one horse, and leffing the races with bundles o' money.

I walking 'bout day and night, all over St. Clair-Oakwood, and still no sight o' the boy.

Then, *bram*! I start hearing horror stories.

"I come out my apartment last Wednesday night to get in my car, and my blasted car not there! It gone. Tow' away!" one fellow say.

A next fellow say, "Be-Christ, if I ever catch a police towing away my car!"

"I don't like this place. It too controlled and full of discipline. Tummuch regulations and laws. A man can't *breathe*. I can't go to the police 'cause I here illegal. No work permit. No job. Now, no car! You park your car, and when you come out in the cold morning to go work at a li'l job, no fucking car!"

"I was up by a little skins one night. I tell the wife I going by Spree. I tack up by Northcliffe at the skin's apartment. I really and truly did intend to spend only a hour.

84

Well, with a few white rums, one thing lead to the next. And when I do so, and open my eyes, morning be-Christ brek, and um is daylight. My arse in trouble now two times. Wife and wuk. I bound down the fire escape, not to be seen, and when I reach ground, no blasted car!"

Stories o' motto-cars tow'way start spreading throughout the St. Clair-Oakwood neighbourhood, just like how the yellow leaves does fall 'pon the grass a certain time o' year. Stories o' fellows getting lay off, no work permit, getting beat up, can't go to the police, in case; and fellows getting lock out by their women — all this gloom start spreading like influenza. The fellows scared. The fellows vex. The fellows angry. And they can't go and complain to the police to find out where their cars is 'cause, as you would understand, the papers not in order, yuh know! And the li'l matter o' *landed* and *recu,* and so on and so forth. . .

They can't even start calling the police "pigs" and "racists" and "criminals." And all this time, nobody can't find the green-hornet boy at all.

Well, a plague of tow'way cars rest so heavy on my mind, even though I don't own no wheels, that I get real concern. 'Cause drunk or sober, blood more thicker than water. . .

"*As man!*"

I hear the voice and I bound round. And look. I see cars. I see Wessindians. I see a police. I see a tow'way truck. And I still don't see nobody I know. But I think I recognize the voice.

"*As man!*"

I bound round again and I see the same things.

"Over here, man!"

God bless my eyesight. Um is the green-hornet man. My friend! Sitting down behind the wheel of *Do Right Towing 24 Hours.* I do so, look! I blink my two eyes. I seeing but I not seeing right. I watching, but I having eyes that see and that watch but they not watching right.

"Um is *me*, man!"

The tow'way truck real pretty. It have in short wave radio. CBC-FM. Stereos. *And* CB. It paint up in black, yellow and white. The green-hornet boy dress off now in overalls and construction hat, cock at a angle on his head, cigar in mouth, and shades on his face, like if he is a dictator from Latin Amurca.

"Remember the plan? The plan I tell you 'bout for making money? Well, I went to my bank and get a loan for this." He tap the door of the tow truck like if he tapping a woman. "And I had a word with a fellow who was a green hornet like me. I is still a green hornet, but I works the afternoon shift. This fellow I know, the ex-green hornet, couldn't take the abuse and the threats to his person of being a hornet, so he open a little place up in Scarborough where he *impounds* the cars I tow'way. And me and he splits the money. I brings in a car, and quick so, um lock up and impounded. If a fellow want back his car, fifty dollars! You want piece o' this action?"

I get real frighten.

"You want to get cut in 'pon this action?"

"But-but-but-but. . ."

"You see that pretty silver-grey Thunderbird park beside that fire hydrand? I watching that car now fifteen minutes. I see the fellow park it and go in the apartment building there. I figure if he coming out soon, he going come out in twenty minutes. I got five more minutes. . ."

I start getting real frighten now. 'Cause I see the car. And the car is the same car that belongst to Goliath, the black Amurcan fellow. I so frighten that I can't talk and warn my green-hornet friend. But even if I could have find words, my tow-truck friend too busy talking and telling me 'bout a piece o' the action, and how easy it is to tow 'way cars that belongst to illegal immigrants, and get money split fifty-fifty, and that to remember the Rockefellers. . .

". . .and I had to laugh one day when I bring in a Cadillac," he tell me, still laughing, as if he was still bringing in the Cadillac. "Appears that my pound friend had a little altercation or difference of opinion with a Murcan man over a car once, so when I appear with the silver-grey Caddy, he get frighten and start telling me that nobody not going maim him or brutalize him or cuss his mother, that before anything like that happen he would go back to Guyana first and pick welts offa reefs or put out oyster pots down by the Georgetown sea wall. . . Look! I got to go. Time up!"

I see him, and I watch him pull off from beside o' me like if he didn't know me, like if I was a fire hydrand. I watch him drive up to the shiny grey Thunderbird car, not mekking no noise, like a real police raiding a Wessindian poker joint after midnight. I see him get out the tow truck, like if he walking on ashes. I see him let down the big iron thing at the back o' the tow truck. First time in my eleven years living here as a semi-legal immigrant that I have see a tow truck that didn't make no noise. I see him bend down and look under the front o' the Thunderbird. I see him wipe his hands. I see him wipe his two hands like a labourer who do a good job does wipe his hands. I see him go round to the back o' the Bird and bend down. He wipe his two hands again. I see him size up the car. I watch him put on the two big canvas gloves on his two hands. I watch him cock the cigar at a more cockier angle, adjust the construction hat, tek off the shades and put them inside his pocket, and I see him take the rope that make out of iron, that look like chain, and hook um on 'pon the gentleman nice, clean-and-polish grey Thunderbird.

I seeing him and I watching him. The boy real professional. I wondering all the time where the boy learn this work. He dance round to the tow truck as if only he was hearing a Barry White slow tune, and press a thing, and the Bird raising up offa the road like if um ready to tek off and fly. I see him press a next thing in the tow truck and the bird stationary but in the air, at a angle, like a Concorde tekking off. I see him bend down again to make sure that the chain o' iron hook on good. I see him wipe his two hands in the big canvas gloves a next time, and I see him slap his two hands, telling me from the distance where I is watching that it is a professional job well done. I think I see the dollar bills registering in his two eyes, too! And I see him tug the chain tight, so the Bird would move off nice and slow, and not jerk nor make no noise, when he ready to tek she to the pound to *impound* she.

And then I see the mountain of the man, tipping toe down the metal fire escape of the apartment building where he was, black shoes shining in the afternoon light, hair slick back and shining more brighter from a "process" hairdo, dress in the same three-piece suit with the pin stripe visible now that the sun was touching the rich material at the right angle o' sheen and shine. And I see, or I think I see, the gentleman take off a diamond-and-gold ring two times, off his right hand, and put them in his pocket. I think I see that, and I see how the hand become big big big like a boxing glove, and I watching but I can't open my mouth nor find voice and words to tell my former green-hornet friend to look over his left shoulder. I seeing but I can't talk o' what I seeing. I find I can't talk. I can only move. A tenseness seize the moment. I do *so*, and point my index finger like a spy telling another spy to don't talk but look behind. But at that very moment the black Amurcan gentleman's hand was already falling on my friend's shoulder. . . .

The Man

THE MAN PASSES THE FIVE OPEN DOORS ON TWO floors that shut as he passes, moving slowly in the dark, humid rooming house. Slowly, pausing every few feet, almost on every other step, he climbs like a man at the end of a double shift in a noisy factory, burdened down also by the weight of time spent on his feet, and by the more obvious weight of his clothes on his fat body, clothes that were seldom cleaned and changed. Heavy with the smell of his body and the weight of paper which he carries with him, in all nine pockets of trousers and jacket and one in his shirt, he climbs, leaving behind an acrid smell of his presence in the already odorous house.

When he first moved into this house, to live in the third-floor room, the landlady was a young wife. She is widowed now, and past sixty. The man smells like the oldness of the house. It is a smell like that which comes off fishermen when they come home from the rum shop after returning from the deep sea. And sometimes, especially in the evening, when the man comes home, the smell stings you and makes you turn your head, as your nostril receives a tingling sensation.

The man ascends the stairs. Old cooking rises and you think you can touch it on walls that have four coats of paint on them, put there by four different previous owners of the house. Or in four moods of decoration. The man pauses again. He inhales. He puts his hands on his hips. Makes a noise of regained strength and determination. And climbs again.

The man is dressed in a suit. The jacket is from a time when shoulders were worn wide and tailored broad. His shoulders are padded high, as his pockets are padded wide by the letters and the pieces of paper with notes on them, and clippings from the *Globe and Mail*, and envelopes with scribbling on them: addresses and telephone numbers. And the printed words he carries in his ten pockets make him look stuffed and overweight and important, and also like a man older than he really is. His hips are like those of a woman who has not always followed her diet to reduce. He meticulously puts on the same suit every day, as he has done for years. He is a man of some order and orderliness. His shirt was once white. He wears only shirts that were white when they were bought. He buys them second-hand from the bins of the Goodwill store on Jarvis Street and wears them until they turn grey. He changes them only when they are too soiled to be worn another day; and then he buys another one from the same large picked-over bins of the Goodwill store.

He washes his trousers in a yellow plastic pail only if a stain is too conspicuous, and presses them under his mattress; and he puts them on before they are completely dry. He walks most of the day, and at eight each night he sits at his stiff, wooden, sturdy-legged table writing letters to men and women all over the world who have distinguished themselves in politics, in government and in universities.

He lives as a bat. Secret and self-assured and self-contained as an island, high above the others in the rooming house; cut off from people, sitting and writing his important personal letters, or reading, or listening to classical music on the radio and the news on shortwave until three or four in the morning. And when morning comes, at eight o'clock he hits the streets, walking in the same two square miles from his home, rummaging through libraries for British and American newspapers, for new words and ideas for letters; then along Bloor Street, Jarvis Street, College Street, and he completes the perimeter at Bathurst Street. His room is the centre of gravity from which he is spilled out at eight each morning in all temperatures and weather, and from which he wanders no farther than these two square miles.

The man used to work as a mover with Maislin Transport in Montreal. Most of the workers came from Quebec and spoke French better than they spoke English. And one day he and a young man dressed in jeans and a red-and-black checkered shirt, resembling a man ready for the woods of lumberjacks and tall trees, were lifting a refrigerator that had two doors; and the man said "Left." He misunderstood the man's English and began to turn left through the small apartment door. He turned old suddenly. His back went out, as the saying goes. And he developed "goadies," a swelling of the testicles so large that they can never be hidden beneath the most restraining jockstrap. That was the end of his moving career.

This former animal of a man, who could lift the heaviest stove if only he was given the correct word, was now a shadow of his former muscle and sinews, with sore back and callused hands, moving slowly through a literary life, with the assistance of a private pension from Maislin Transport. He has become a different kind of animal now, prowling during the daytime through shelves of books in stores and in libraries, and visiting slight acquaintances as if they were friends whenever he smelled a drink or a meal; and attending public functions.

His pension cheque came every month at the same time,

written in too much French for the rude bank teller, who said each time he presented it, even after two years, "Do you have some *identification*?"

He used to be sociable. He would nod his head to strangers, flick his eyes on the legs of women and at the faces of foreign-language men on College Street, all the way west of Spadina Avenue. He would even stop to ask for a light, and once or twice for a cigarette, and become confused in phrase-book phrases of easy, conversational Greek, Portuguese and Italian.

Until one evening. He was walking on a shaded street in Forest Hill Village when a policeman looked through the window of his yellow cruiser, stopped him in his wandering tracks and said, "What the hell 're you doing up here, *boy*?" He had been walking and stopping, unsure along this street, looking at every mansion which seemed larger than the one before, when he heard the brutal voice. "Git in! Git your black ass in here!"

The policeman threw open the rear door of the cruiser. The man looked behind him, expecting to see a delinquent teenager who had earned the policeman's raw hostility. The man was stunned. There was no other person on the street. But somehow he made the effort to walk to the cruiser. The door was slammed behind him. The policeman talked on a stuttering radio and used figures and numbers instead of words, and the man became alarmed at the policeman's mathematical illiteracy. And then the cruiser sped off, scorching the peace of Forest Hill, burning rubber on its shaded quiet streets.

The cruiser stopped somewhere in the suburbs. He thought he saw Don Mills on a sign post. It stopped here, with the same temperamental disposition as it had stopped the first time in Forest Hill Village. The policeman made no further conversation of numerals and figures with the radio. He merely said, *"Git!"* The man was put out three miles from any street or intersection that he knew.

It was soon after this that he became violent. He made three pillows into the form of a man. He found a second-hand tunic and a pair of trousers that had a red stripe in them, and a hat that had a yellow band instead of a red one, and he dressed up the pillows and transformed them into a dummy of a policeman. And each morning at seven when he woke up, and late at night before he went to bed, after he washed out his mouth with salt water, he kicked the "policeman" twice — once in the flat feathery section where a man's testicles would be, and again at the back of the pillow in the dummy's ass. His hatred did not disappear with the blows. But soon he forgot about the effigy and the policeman.

Today he had been roaming the streets, like every day, tearing pieces of information from the *Globe and Mail* he took from a secretary's basket at the CBC, from *Saturday Night* and *Canadian Forum* magazines. And the moment he reached his attic room, he would begin to compose letters to great man and women around the world, inspired by the bits of information he had gathered.

And now, as he climbs, the doors of the roomers on each floor close as he passes, like an evil wind. But they close too late, for his scent and the wind of his presence have already touched them.

With each separation and denial, he is left alone in the dim light to which he is accustomed, and in the dust on the stairs; and he guides his hand along the shining bannister, the same sheen as the wallpaper, stained with the smells and specks of cooking. He walks slowly because the linoleum on the stairs is shiny too, and dangerous and tricky under the feet.

Now, on his last flight to his room for the night, his strength seems to leave his body, and he pauses and rests his hands, one on the bannister and the other on his right hip.

The cheque from Montreal will arrive tomorrow.

He feels the bulkiness of the paper in his pockets, and the weight of his poverty in this country he never grew to love. There was more love in Barbados. On many a hot afternoon, he used to watch his grandfather rest his callused hand on his hip as he stood in a field of endless potatoes, a field so large and quiet and cruel that he thought he was alone in the measureless sea of green waves, and not on a plantation. Alone perhaps now too, in the village, in the country, because of his unending work of bending his back to pull up the roots, and returning home when everyone else is long in bed.

And now he, the grandson, not really concerned with that stained ancestry, not really comparing himself with his grandfather, stands for a breath-catching moment on this landing in this house in which he is a stranger. He regards his room as the country. It is strange and familiar. It is foreign, yet it is home. It is dirty. And at the first signs of summer and warmth, he would go down on his hands and knees in what would have been an unmanly act and scrub the small space outside his door, and the four or five steps he had to climb to reach it. He would drop soap into the water, and still the space around the door remained dirty. The house had passed that stage when it could be cleaned. It had grown old like a human body. And not even ambition and cleanliness could purify it of this scent. It could be cleaned only by burning. But he had become accustomed to the dirt, as he was accustomed to the thought of burning. In the same way, he had become accustomed to the small room which bulged, like his ten pockets, with the possessions of his strange literary life.

He is strong again. Enough to climb the last three or four steps and take out his keys on the shining ring of silver, after putting down the plastic bag of four items he had bought through the express check-out of Dominion around the corner, and then the collection of newspapers —

two morning and two afternoon and two evening editions. He flips each key over, and it makes a dim somersault, until he reaches the last key on the ring which he knows has to be the key he's looking for.

Under the naked light bulb he had opened and shut, locked and unlocked this same blue-painted door when it was painted green and red and black, so many times that he thought he was becoming colour-blind. But he could have picked out the key even if he was blind; for it was the only key in the bunch which had the shape of the fleur de lys at its head. He went through all the keys on the ring in a kind of elimination process. It was his own private joke. A ritual for taking up time.

He spent time as if he thought it would not end: walking along College Street and Spadina Avenue when he was not thinking of letters to be written; looking at the clusters of men and women from different countries at the corner of Bathurst and Bloor; at the men passing their eyes slowly over the breasts and backsides of the women; at the women shopping at Dominion and the open-air stalls, or amongst the fibres of cheap materials and dresses, not quite pure silk, not one hundred percent cotton, which they tore as they searched for and tore from each other's hands to get at cheaper prices than those advertised at Honest Ed's bargain store. And he would watch how these women expressed satisfaction with their purchases in their halting new English.

And now in the last few months, along those streets he had walked and known, all of a sudden the names on stores and the signs on posts appeared in the hieroglyphics of Chinese. Or Japanese? He no longer felt safe, tumbling in the warmth and shouts of a washing machine in a public laundromat in this technicoloured new world of strangers.

He had loved those warm months and those warm people before their names and homes were written in signs. They were real until someone turned them into Chinese characters which he could not read. And he spent the warm months of summer writing letters to the leaders of the world, in the hope of getting back a reply, no matter how short or impersonal, with their signatures, which he intended to sell to the highest bidder.

He came from a colony, a country and a culture where the written word spelled freedom. An island where the firm touch of the pen on paper meant freedom. Where the pen gripped firmly in the hand was sturdier than a soldier holding a gun, and which meant liberation. And the appearance of words on paper, the meaning and transformation they gave to the paper, and the way they rendered the paper priceless, meant that he could now escape permanently from the profuse sweat and the sharp smell of perspiration on the old khaki trousers and the thick-smelling flannel worn next to the skin. This sweat was the uniform, and had been the profession of poor black grandfathers. Now pen and paper mean the sudden and unaccountable and miraculous disappearance from a colonial tradition where young bodies graduated from the play and games and beaches of children into the dark, steamy and bee-droning caverns and caves of warehouses in which sat white men in white drill suits and white cork hats, their white skin turning red from too much rum and too much sun, and from their too-deep appetites for food and local women. For years before this graduation, he could find himself placed like a lamp post, permanent and blissful in one job, in one spot, in one position, until perhaps a storm came, or a fierce hurricane, and felled him like the chattels of houses and spewed him into the gutter.

So he learned the power of the *word*. And kept close to it. When others filled the streets and danced in a Caribana festival and wore colours hot as summer in a new spring of life, this man remained in his isolation; and he cut himself off from those frivolous, ordinary pleasures of life that had surrounded his streets for years, just as the immigrants surrounded the open-air Kensington Market. He thought and lived and expressed himself in this hermitage of solitary joy, writing letters to President de Gaulle, President Carter, Willy Brandt (whose name he never learned to spell), to Mao Tse Tung, Dr. Martin Luther King and Prime Minister Indira Gandhi.

The few acquaintances he called friends and met for drinks on the eighteenth-floor bar of the Park Plaza Hotel, and those he visited and talked with and drank with in their homes, all thought he was mad. And perhaps he was mad. Perhaps his obsession with the word had sent him off.

The persons to whom he wrote were all unknown to him. He did not care for their politics or their talent. But he made a fortune out of time spent in addressing them. It was an international intrusion on their serious lives: *Dear Prime Minister, I saw your name and picture in the Toronto Globe and Mail this morning. I must say I was most impressed by some of the things you have said. You are one of the most indispensable personages in this western world. This western world would come to its end of influence were it not for you. You and you alone can save it and save us. Long may you have this power. Yours very sincerely, William Jefferson.*

"Look what I pulled off!" he told Alonzo. He held the glass of cold beer bought for him on the account of friendship, and a smile came to his face. The smile was the smile of literary success. He had just promised Alonzo that he would defray all his loans with the sale of his private correspondence. A smile came to Alonzo's face. It was the smile of accepted social indebtedness. "The university would just *love* to get its hands on this!" *This* was the reply from the Prime Minister: a plain white post card on which was written, *Thank you very much, Mr. Jefferson, for your thoughtfulness.*

He would charge the university one hundred dollars for the reply from Prime Minister Gandhi. Perhaps he could sell them his entire correspondence! Why not? Even publish them in *The Private Correspondence of William Jefferson with the Great Men and Great Women of the Twentieth Century.*

Alonzo did not know whether to continue smiling or laugh right out. He could not decide if his friend was slightly off the head. He needed more proof. The letter from Mrs. Gandhi, which he did not show, could supply the proof. But it was a man's private business, a man's private correspondence; and not even the postman who delivered it had the right to see it. If this correspondence went on, Alonzo thought, who knows, perhaps one day he may be drinking beer and associating with a man of great fame, a famous man of letters, hounded by universities to get a glimpse of this correspondence. . . .

While the man is trying to unlock his door, the urge overtakes him. The keyhole had not answered the key. And the urge to pee swells over his body like a high wave. This urge would overcome him almost always when a porcelain oval hole was not immediately available. It would take him into its grip and turn his entire body into a cramping, stuttering muscle-bound fist. Always on the wrong side of the street, too.

He was on Bloor Street once, in that stretch of shops and stores and restaurants where women wear furs and carry merchandise in shopping bags with Creeds and Holt Renfrew and Birks proclaimed on them, where the restaurants look like country clubs and the shops like chapels and banks, where he could not get the nerve to enter the stained-glass door with heraldry on it, jerk a tense glance in *that* direction and receive the direction to *there* or get a sign to show him the complicated carpeted route to *washrooms* printed on a brass plate. Not dressed the way he was. Not without giving some explanation. Not without alarming the waitresses dressed more like nurses and the waiters who looked like fashion models.

Once he dashed into Holt Renfrew. It was the last desperate haven. The water was heavy on his nerves, on his bladder. His eyes were red and watery. He barely had strength to speak his wish. Experience with this urge had cautioned him, as he stood before the glass case of ladies' silk underwear, that to open his mouth at that moment, when the association of this urge with ladies' panties was in full view, meant a relaxation of his grip on the water inside him. Then it would pour out onto the carpeted floor of Persian silence, perhaps even dribble onto the feet of the young clerk whose legs he could see beneath the thinness of her almost transparent dress.

The young woman saw his stiffness and posture, and with a smile and a wave, showed him the nearest haven. It had *Employees Only* inscribed on the shining brass. When he was finished, he could not move immediately. The loss of weight and water was like the loss of energy. "Have a good day, sir!" Her smile was brighter then.

He was still outside his room. The key was still in the hole. He did not have the strength to go down two flights of stairs to the second-floor bathroom beside the room of the woman who lived on welfare.

To have to go down now, with this weight making his head heavier, did something with his hand and the key turned.

He was safe inside his room. Relieved and safe. He did it in the pail. He keeps this pail in a corner, under the table, on which is a two-ringed hot plate. In times of urgency, he uses it, and in times of laziness and late at night. He adds soap flakes to the steaming liquid to hide its smell and composition, and when he carries the plastic pail down, the woman on welfare cannot smell or detect his business. He relishes his privacy.

Sometimes he has no flakes of soap, so he drops a pair of soiled underwear into the urine and walks with it, pretending there is no smell; and if the coast is clear, he bolts the lock on the bathroom door and does his business and laundry like a man hiding from his superstition.

He had heard that a famous Indian politician used to drink his own pee. And it overcame him.

He is safe inside his room. He breathes more easily now. He is home. His room relaxes him. It is like a library of a man obsessed with books and eccentric about the majesty of books.

Red building blocks which he stole two at a time are placed in fours at each end of the white-painted three-ply shelves. And the shelves end, as a scaffold should, at the end of available space, the ceiling. The same construction occupies all four walls. There are books of all sizes, all topics, all tastes.

The space between the bottom shelf and the floor is crammed with newspapers which are now yellow. There are magazines with their backs missing through frequent use. Each new magazine goes into the space which can get no larger. Statements of great political and international significance, the photograph of a man or a woman to be written to, are torn out from their sources and pinned to the three-ply shelves with common pins; and there are framed photographs of writers whom this man regards as the great writers of the world. No one else has heard of them.

He has collected relics of his daily passage throughout the city, in the same two square miles, not going beyond this perimeter. He has never again ventured into that part of the suburbs where the policeman had picked him up.

Among his relics are jars and bottles, and one beautiful piece of pottery that looks as if it had been unearthed in an archeological digging somewhere in the distant world. It is brown and has a mark like antiquity around its swelling girth; and where it stands on an old trunk that could have belonged to a sea captain, or to an immigrant from Europe or the West Indies, large enough to transport memories and possessions from a poorer life to this new country, this little brown jug gives age and seriousness to the other useless but priceless pieces in his room.

In all the jars and bottles, and in this brown "antique" jug, are dried branches of trees, flowers, sprigs and brambles. Dead beyond recognition.

The man collects dead things. Leaves and brambles and flowers and twigs. And he must like this death in things because there is nothing that lives in his room. Nothing but the man himself. He does not see them as dead things, or as meaning death.

He has five clocks. They are all miraculously set at the same, precise time, with not a second's difference. Every morning, using the time on the CBC radio as his standard and barometer, he checks and re-checks each of his five clocks; and when this is done, he sits on his old-fashioned, large and comfortable couch, upholstered in green velvet that now has patches like sores in the coat of a dog, with knobs of dull mahogany at the ends where the fingers touch, or rest, or agitate (if he is writing or thinking about a letter to an important personage in the world). He would sit here, now that he has set his time, and listen to the ticking, secure ordering of the meaning of time; pretending he is back home in the island that consumes time, where all the clocks ticked at various dispositions and carried different times. Canada has taught him one important discipline. And he has learned about time. He has learned always to be *in* time.

Paper bags are stuffed between books, folded in their original creases and placed there, anxious for when they can be used a second time. A cupboard in the room is used as a clothes closet, a pantry and a storeroom. It contains more paper bags of all sizes, of all origins, from all supermarkets; but most are from Dominion. They are tied and made snug and tidy by elastic bands whose first use he has obviously forgotten. On the bottom shelf of the cupboard are plastic bags imprinted with barely visible names of stores and shops, folded in a new improvised crease and placed into a large brown paper bag.

All this time, he is walking the four short lengths of floor bordered by his books, stopping in front of one shelf, running his fingers absentmindedly over the titles of books. The linoleum floor is punctuated by the nails in his shoes that walk up and down, late into the night of thoughtfulness, of worrying about a correct address or a correct salutation. Now he stands beside a large wooden table made by immigrants or early settlers on farms, in the style of large sturdy legs the size and shape of their own husky peasant form. This table does not move. It cannot move. On it he has storeroomed his food and his drinks, his "eatables and drinkables," and it functions as his pantry of dishes and pots and pans. At one end of the table is the gas hot plate, the only implement for cooking that is allowed in this illegally-small living space.

On the hot plate is a shining aluminium saucepan battered around its girth by temper, hunger and burned rice.

He uncovers the saucepan. The food is old. Its age, two or three days, has thickened its smell, and makes it look like wet cement. The swollen black-eyed peas sit permanently among hunks of pig tails. He is hungry all of a sudden. These two urges, peeing and eating, come upon him without notice and with no regard to the last time he has eaten or peed. So he digs a "pot spoon" into the heart of the thick drying cement of food and uproots the swollen hunks of pig tails whose oily taste brings water and nostalgia to his eyes, and he half shuts his eyes to eat the first mouthful.

He replaces the lid. He puts the "pot spoon" between the saucepan rim and the lid, and pats the battered side of the saucepan the way a trainer would pat a horse that has just won on a long-shot bet.

He takes off his jacket. It is two sizes too large. Then he takes off his red woollen sweater, and another one of cotton, and long-sleeved; and then a third, grey, long-sleeved, round-necked and marked *Property of the Athletic Department, University of Toronto.*

He is a man of words, and the printed claim of ownership on his third pullover never ceases to amaze and impress him.

Stripped now of his clothes, he is left in a pair of grey long johns. And it is in these that he walks about the wordy room, ruminating as he struggles late into the night to compose the correct arrangement of words that would bring him replies from the pens of the great. Sometimes his own words do not flow as easily as he would wish. And this literary constipation aborts the urge to pee. At such times he runs to his Javex box, where he keeps all the replies he has ever received. He reads them now, praying for an easier movement of words from the bowels of his brain.

Dear Mr. Jefferson, Thank you for your letter.

That was all from one great personage. But it was good enough. It was a reply. And an official one at that. A rubber stamp of the signature tells you of the disinterest or the thick appointment book of the sender, that perhaps the sender does not understand the archival significance of the letter he has received from Mr. William Jefferson.

This is to acknowledge receipt of your letter.

Another reply from a great personage. Even the stamp, print and address are reproductions of the original. But the man believes that some value lies even in this impersonal reply.

Dear Mr. Jefferson, We are very glad to know that, as a Barbadian, you have introduced us to the archives of the University of Toronto, which is considering maintaining a Barbados collection. We wish you every success in your significant venture.

This is his most valuable letter. It is signed by someone who lives! A human hand has signed it. But he cannot untangle the name from its spidery script. He does not know who has replied to him. For typed beneath the script is only the person's official position: *Secretary*.

He understands more than any other living person the archival importance of these letters. And he treasures them within a vast imagination of large expectations, in this large brown box which contained Javex for bleaching clothes before it fell into his possession.

He has been nervous all week. And this nervousness erupted in strong urges to pee, strong and strange even for his weak bladder. The nervousness was linked to the price of his collection. This afternoon he had spoken to someone at the university. Over the telephone the voice told him, "Of course! Of course, Mr. Jefferson. We'll be interested in seeing your collection." It was a polite reply, like the written ones in his Javex box. But as a man obsessed by his relics, who attaches great significance to their esoteric value, he inflates that significance. He is also a man who would read an offer to purchase in a polite reply from the university. He is a man who hears more words than those that are spoken.

He starts to count his fortune. This letter to him from a living Prime Minister would be the basis of his fortune. His friend Alonzo would get a free round of beer at the Park Plaza roof bar. He would pay his rent six months in advance. He would have more time to spend on his private correspondence with the great men and women of the world.

He holds the Prime Minister's letter in his hand and examines the almost invisible water marks on which it is typed. He studies the quality of the official stationery made in Britain and used by the West Indies, and compares it to that of Canada and the United States. He decides that the British and West Indies knew more about prestigious stationery. He continues to feel the paper between big thumb and two adjoining fingers, rubbing and rubbing and feeling a kind of orgasm coming on; and in this trance, he reads another letter.

Dear Mr. Jefferson, Thank you for your kind and thoughtful letter. Yours, Prime Minister's Office.

Above this line, "Margaret Thatcher" is stamped in fading ink. Still, it is a mark on history; "a first" from a poor woman whom history had singled out to be great.

When he is in his creative mood, he moves like a man afraid to cause commotion in a room in which he is a guest, like a man moving amongst bric-a-brac, priceless mementos of glass and china and silver locked in a glass cabinet. He moves about his room soundlessly, preparing his writing materials and deepening his mood for writing.

His stationery is personalized. *William Jefferson, Esquire* is printed in bold letters at the top of the blue page. And below that, his address. He writes with a fountain pen. And when he fills it from the bottle of black ink, he always smiles when the pen makes its sucking noise. This sucking noise takes him back years to another room in another country when he formed his first letters. And he likes the bottle that contains the ink. It has a white label, with a squeezed circle like an alert eye; and through this eye, through the middle of this eye, is an arrow which pierces it. *Parker super quink ink. Permanent black.* It suggests strength and longevity. It is like his life: determined and traditional, poised outside the mainstream but fixed in habit and custom. Whenever he uses this fountain pen, his index finger and the finger next to that, and his thumb, bear the verdict and the evidence of this permanent blackness. This *noire*. He sometimes wishes that he could use the language of Frenchmen who slip words and the sounds of those words over their tongues like raw oysters going down the throat!

"What a remarkable use of the tongue the French have! That back of the throat sensation!" he told Alonzo one afternoon, but in such a way as if he were speaking to the entire room in the Park Plaza Hotel bar.

Noire.

Many years ago, in 1955, the minute his feet touched French soil at Dorval in Quebec, the first greeting he heard was *"Noire!"* The sound held him in its grip, and changed his view of ordinary things, and made him fastidious and proper and suspicious. The only word he retained was *noire.* It was not a new word to him. For years even before that greeting, and in Barbados on a Sunday afternoon after the heavy midday meal, he used to sit at the back door looking out onto the cackling of hens, one of which he had eaten earlier, inhaling with the freshness of stomach and glorious weather the strong smell of Nugget shoe polish as he lathered it on his shoes and on his father's shoes and his mother's shoes and his grandfather's shoes. So he had already dipped his hands into *noire* long before Canada.

He had known *noire* for years. But no one had addressed him as *noire.*

He likes the *noire* of the ink he uses, as he liked the *noire* in the Nugget which gave his shoes longer life and made them immortal and left its proud, industrious and indelible stain on his fingers.

Tomorrow the University of Toronto is coming to buy his papers. He runs his hands over his letters in the Javex box, hundreds of them, and thinks of money and certified cheques. He empties all his pockets and puts the papers on the table. He picks up each piece like a man picking flesh from a carcass of bones. Who should he write to tonight?

The silent books around him, their words encased in covers, do not offer advice. But he knows what they would answer. He finds it difficult to concentrate. Tomorrow is too near. The money from his papers, cash or certified cheque, is too close at hand. He spends time spending it in his mind. And the things contained in tomorrow, like the things contained in his Javex box, have at last delivered him, just as his articulate use of the pen confirmed the value of the word and delivered him from the raving crowds of new immigrants. He has gained peace and a respectable distance from those aggressive men and women because of his use of the word.

"Should I write to the President of Yale University?"

The books, thick in their shelves around him, and few of which he has read from cover to cover, all these books remain uncommunicative and have no words of advice.

"Should I write to President Reagan?"

His five electric clocks continue to keep constant time, and in their regulated determination, refuse to disclose a tick of assistance.

"The Prime Minister of Barbados?"

Barbados is no longer home. Home, he had told Alonzo ten years ago, "is where I pee and eat and write."

He gets up and turns on the flame of the hot plate under the saucepan. "While the grass is growing, the horse is starving," he tells the saucepan. He smiles at his own wisdom. The heat makes the saucepan crackle. "While the grass is growing. . ." The thin saucepan makes a smothered crackling sound. The hot plate seems to be melting the coagulated black-eyed peas and rice and pig tails. The hot plate is crackling as if it is intent upon melting the cheap alloy of the saucepan and turning the meal into soft hot lead, and then spreading its flame over the letters on the table, and then the table itself, and then the room. He lowers the flame.

"Fire cleans everything," he tells the hot plate. The saucepan stops laughing with the heat. His meal has settled down to being re-cooked.

But he is soon smelling things. The nostalgia of food and the perspiration from his mother's forehead as she cooked the food, and the strong, rich smell of pork. He smells also the lasting wetness of flannel shirts worn in the fields back on the small island.

He gets accustomed to these smells. And he thinks again of new correspondence since all these on the table before him would be gone by tomorrow, sold, archived among other literary riches. A hand-rubbing enthusiasm and contentment brings a smile to his face.

"I'll write the Prime Minister of Barbados!"

The smell comes up again. With the help of the smell, he is back on the small island, witnessing spires of blue smoke pouring out from each small castle of patched tin and rotting wood where his village stood. He can hear the waves and the turbulent sea, so much like the turbulence of water he boiled in the same thin-skin saucepan to make tea. As he thinks back, his eyes pass over used tea bags spread in disarray, an action caught in the midst of an important letter when he would sometimes drop a used tea bag into the yellow plastic pail.

Dear Prime Minister. . .

He reaches over to the hot plate and raises the flame. He sees it change from yellow to blue, and smiles. "The horse is starving. . ."

Certain important universities have asked me to act as a liaison to encourage you to submit your. . .

The fragile aluminium saucepan is losing its battle in the heat of warming the food. But it is the smell. The smell takes his mind off the letter, and off the great sums of money, cash and certified cheques. He is a boy again, running home from school, colliding with palings and dogs and the rising smells of boiled pork reddened in tomatoes and bubbling over rice like the thick tar which the road workers poured over a raw road under construction.

He can taste his country now. Clearly. And see the face of the Prime Minister, greedy to make a name for himself in a foreign institution of higher learning, and obtain foreign currency for his foreign account.

. . . I have lived a solitary life, apart from the demonstrations and protests of the mainstream of immigrants. I have become a different man. A man of letters. I am more concerned with cultural things, radio, books and libraries, than with reports. . .

Something is wrong with his pen. The flow is clogged and constricted, just like when he's caught with his pants up in a sudden urge to pee, and having forced it inwards, cannot get it outwards. And he gets up and heads downstairs. Just as he's moving away from his door, still on the first three or four steps going down, he turns back. "My pen is my penis," he tells the door.

He picks up the yellow plastic pail. He throws a shirt and underwear into the brown stagnant water. It looks like stale beer. Before he goes through the door again, he picks up the unfinished letter to the Prime Minister of Barbados, and in his long johns, armed with pail and paper, he creeps out.

The stairs are still dim. And he smiles. He moves down slowly, hoping that when he reaches the second floor the woman on welfare who occupies the toilet longer than any other tenant would not be there.

The saucepan has now begun to boil, although there are more solids than liquids within its thin frame. Popcorn comes into his mind. He doesn't even eat popcorn! He doesn't even go to the movies! The saucepan is turning red at the bottom. If he was in his room, he could not tell where the saucepan's bottom began and where the ring of the hot plate ended.

He thinks of roast corn as he reaches the closed door of the only bathroom in the house. He stands. He listens. He smells. He inhales. And he exhales. He puts his hand on the door and pushes gently, and the door opens with a small creak. He stands motionless, alarmed to see that the bathroom is indeed empty. Where is the woman on welfare?

... at night, back home, in the crop season when the sugar canes are cut and harvested, they burn the corn over coals. ...

Right then, above his head, the saucepan explodes. He doesn't hear it. The black-eyed peas and rice burst out, pelting the cover before it, and the table top is splattered like careless punctuation marks. It falls on his fine blue stationery.

The explosion comes just as he holds the yellow pail at a tilt, over the growling toilet bowl. In the same hand as the pail is the unfinished letter. The urine is flowing into the bowl and he stands thinking, when he sees the first clouds of smoke crawling down the stairs, past the open bathroom door.

The smoke becomes heavier and makes tears come into his eyes. He is crying and passing his hands in front of his face, trying to clear a passage from the second floor, through the thickening smoke rising like high waves. Up and up he goes, no faster than when he entered the house that afternoon, struggling through the smoke until he reaches the steps in front of his door. And as he gets there, it seems as if all the books, all the letters, all the bags of plastic and paper shout at once in an even greater explosion.

Before he can get downstairs to call for help from the woman on welfare, he thinks he hears all five of his clocks alarming. And then, in the way a man who has been struck by a deadening blow waits for the second one to land, he stands, expecting the five clocks to do something else. It is then that he hears one clock striking the hour. He counts aloud until he reaches eight, and then he refuses to count any longer.

On One Leg

ALEXANDER CAME INTO THE BEVERAGE ROOM like a soldier. Like a general in full dress. With his chest full and broad with the ribbons and medals of his fifty years of experience and battles. Alexander's battles were fought on the battle-scarred field of everyday life. He walked with a heavy step. And as he walked, you knew he was a man of some substance. He looked so. Perhaps it was the experience that decorated his face with lines and age. This same experience had ruffled his hair with the fingers of its tragedies. And it had marked his face in circles and crow's-feet, like the boulders crawling at the bottom of a mighty long and slow river would have marked the river.

When he sat down, his body from his waist up to his neck was as stiff as a wooden leg. His head would lean forward, always his head, as if he regarded any aspect of the conversation of his drinking friends to be so important. In the men's beverage room of the Selby Hotel, where he drank every afternoon straight from work with a ritualistic regularity, his head would follow the meandering slurring vocabulary of his friends, like a child's pencil following the outlines of a picturebook drawing.

All the men in the Selby liked Alexander. He was like a general to all of them. They thought he was a bit aloof, but they knew that he liked them too. He carried in his heart a feeling for them that was equalled only by the love and affection which soldiers who have survived wars and close calls have known. The men in the beverage room were like soldiers to Alexander.

He was always anxious to get there. And when he sat down, it seemed as if he had prepared his system and his appetite the whole day, from nine until five in the afternoon, just for these few hours of being together among men.

"I've been with men," he told his tired, complaining, callous-handed wife one night as he entered the moth-balled house after an evening of drinking beer that stretched out too long, long as the tales of his battles at work, and in the mine in northern Ontario where he had worked for some time. But this did not appease her. She did not know anything about men, she said.

"They was *men*," he insisted.

He would talk to them like men talked to other men. He would talk about his job, and he would dress his job in important phrases and give tragedy, if not drama, to the sorting of letters which bored him eight hours a day in the main post office downtown, but which he would never admit to his drinking companions. As far as they were concerned, it was a job, like tactical manoeuvres. As far as he was concerned, he was like a general putting little flags of many different colours on a very complicated map, and directing from this apparently simple movement of flags and hands a theatre of combat whose proportions were great enough to involve the lives of many thousands, of many millions of people: the entire population of Toronto.

"You have to observe," he was telling his friends one afternoon, "you should see me in that occupation. There's one thing about handling the nation's mails." And he would sip a bit of his beer and allow them to grasp the full

114

meaning of his last words. "You have to be a man of a certain level of intelligence and education to work in this job I have." And he would again pause and permit them time to raise their glasses to their heads, and he would not continue until each man had swallowed, along with his drink, all that he had said up till then. "Now, I'm a man who didn't go to university. But I have seen college kids come to work there in the summer, in the post office, and this job that I do, it gives them a hell of a lotta trouble just to learn the fundamentals."

All the men would breathe easier and they would look important, as if *their* jobs were shining in their faces, because none of them had gone to university either; because many of them had not even finished high school. But each one of them could tell a similar story of a university student to whom they had taught a summer job.

"It could be a serious thing. Imagine. The slightest mistake, the slightest miscalculation, and a letter could go to the wrong person. And people stealing so much nowadays! They could even open a letter and take out the money, if it had any, 'cause people nowadays, particularly the young ones, the ones you see in Yorkville with long hair, hippies, you understand what I'm talking about. . ."

The men would all nod their heads. They understood. They understood because they had all felt this way about the young men with long hair walking about Toronto "like living deads," as Alexander called them.

"I would take on the youngest o' them right now," he said on another afternoon, "and I lay a sawbuck on it that he couldn't throw me!"

The men nodded and cheered with their eyes. Alexander was talking like a real, honest, hard-working man. "Not one o' them! If I had a son still living, who'd be twenty this year — ten years he died — but if he himself was living today, *he* couldn't throw me! And I am his father. I am a man now, going into my. . ." But he thought better of the idea and did not tell them how old he was. "A man my age is no pup," he said with a grin.

The men grinned too. They nodded their heads faster and more vigorously to show him, like a kind of illustration of sympathy, that they too were old men, but strength and vigour and marrow hadn't gone out of their bodies, their spirits or their bones.

"Yeah!" one of them, Joe, said a bit too loud, for they were sitting at a round table, close together as poker players. "Yeah, Lex! Men!"

He was the only one who dared to call Alexander "Lex." And he too fell silent and allowed Alexander to fill up the beverage room with the real meaning of sweat and sinews and muscles and hard-nailed boots and potato chips, chomped like pieces of dried bramble.

Alexander liked these beer-drinking gatherings. Whatever problem he might have had at work would be set aside, just as he always pushed the loaded ashtray of spit-stained cigars and plain-tipped cigarettes from in front of his seat and in his easy and unstudied movement made it seem as if the ashtray was the last fistful of letters placed correctly into the pigeonhole at the post office.

He had therefore successfully pigeonholed one branch of his slowly moving life, and had skipped enthusiastically into the turbulence of this artery which bubbled in the beverage room of the Selby Hotel. He would rub his hands together like two slabs of board covered with sandpaper, slap them firmly but not loudly, and not in any real rhythm of jubilation, but as if to say, Good! Time for a good, cold beer.

He came into the beverage room this Friday afternoon and brushed aside Joe's ashtray that was in front of his usual seat, although nobody had ever decided upon any order of seating. He slapped his callouses and said, "One

116

here, Bill!" One was his favourite drink. Beer. And Bill was the waiter. It was not his real name, but they had all christened him Bill. It saved them the complication and the mincing of tongue and beer and words and enunciation to pronounce *Sudzynowski*, which Bill told them in his halting English was the name his Polish godmother had given him back in the days across the Atlantic Ocean when he was a baby.

"*Fairy*godmother!" Alexander jeered with his mouth full of broth and beer and smoke. "Eh? Eh? Eh? *Fairy*-godmother!" he screamed with laughter, the beer dripping down his mouth. Sudzynowski began to teach them how to pronounce his name correctly, for he preferred to be called by it. But they laughed and he decided to forget it.

"Ahh! What the hell? We'll call you Bill," Alexander said. The others nodded in agreement. "'Smore friendly. What you say, Bill? What you say, fellas? You see, we're a friendly people, eh? Eh?"

Sudzynowski nodded his head and shrugged his shoulders and went away saying something in Polish. It was not very friendly.

"Another one here, Bill," Alexander said five minutes later when the waiter was within hearing distance. "Bag o' chips while you're at it. Worked like a slave today, fellas. All day. I want to tell you fellas something, something I never told you before in all the months we been joking and drinking together in this place. Pack o' Exports! A's! Worked like a slave today, and all the time I watching some young fellas sneaking off to the can to get a rest and a smoke. There I was with not a man, not none o' them young fellas man enough to match me, to stand up to me. Those bastards with long hair, they won't take a bath, got the whole goddamn post office smelling like a urinal in the train station, I swear to God! If my boy was still living, and he ever showed me his kisser with that kind o' hairdo,

I smack him one!" Bill, the re-christened waiter, was approaching with the beer and cigarettes. "Eh? Eh? Eh? What you say, Bill? You like hippies? You're a Polack hippie, ain't ya? Eh?"

Bill smiled, and inside his smile he wished them dead. He placed the beer courteously on the shining black table-top, set Alexander's chips and cigarettes before him, smiled again, waited for the ten-cent tip he always got from Alexander — nothing more, nothing less, regardless of the amount of beer he drank — and then left, cursing Alexander and all the men at the table, in his mind, in his own language.

"Any o' you fellas ever worked in a mine? I mean a mine. Underground. You go down on that lift five o'clock every morning to work your shift, your lunch pail in your hand, your heart in your goddamn mouth, though you can't show it to the other fellas, and you know, as your buddies know, that one o' these days none o' you might see the light o' day again when that shift ends. Never again. That's what I call *work*. Well, I was a miner once. Twenty years of it. After the war. Worked in the MacIntyre. Timmins. Best goddamn gold mine in the world one time. That's my opinion. Best goddamn high-grade miner you see sitting right in front of you. Worked like a bitch in those days. Made money too. Good money. Spent every goddamn penny on women, whisky and poker. But I had me a ball! I mean a mine! MacIntyre. In Timmins. Wasn' a woman in town who escaped my wrath!"

The men roared. The waiter, standing by the counter, looked up from watching television.

"Used to shack up with a Indian woman in them days. Best goddamn woman in the North too! In the world. Kind as anything to me. Worked like a bastard and ate like a horse, I did. Shot me a moose twice every winter. My Indian woman acted as my guide all through the bush.

118

Like say for two months. November, December, January, February and March we lived like a goddamn bear inside that shack we called our home. Me and my goddamn woman. *Lived!* I was a man then. Screwed like a bitch too. Them days I had my wife living in a town fifteen miles south. Porcupine. Lived like a man, I did!"

He whetted his tale with a large draught of beer and dried it with a smack. The others, waiting on his cue, raised their glasses to their lips; and as they settled down to listen again, they wiped their melting moustaches of beads and beer.

Alexander made them cry and he made them bawl with laughter and sympathy at his stories of the North. They laughed at his jokes about the women he had conquered like a real general, and they saw him as a general. He was a great man, a great goddamn buddy, they said in words and in looks. And they would always wait for him, should they arrive at the Selby before him; and they'd order just one beer each and nurse it until Alexander came through the door and into the darkened beverage room already noisy before he entered, with the footsteps of sand on the floor and television soap operas which none of them watched except Joe, though they insisted it always be on.

He would come in like a soldier. And when he sat down, it seemed as if they had gathered their breaths and attention in one long intake. And they would wait until he was settled in his scraping chair. He told them, careening over the years of his life in the Canadian army, of his conquests, especially his personal conquests of women in Italy, in North Africa, in the Suez and in Britain. But the woman he talked most about was his Indian woman from Timmins.

"One night my missus sneaked up on me! And, god-damn, fellas. . .well, I don't have to tell you the rest!" They laughed like men would laugh at this kind of joke; and they blamed his wife, whom none of them knew, for being so goddamn thoughtless as to sneak up on him. A man like Alexander deserved a better wife, a more thoughtful wife, a wife who could understand such things, who could understand that she was living in the company and sleeping in the bed of a great man, a general.

"Women and wives can be clumsy sometimes," Joe said.

Alexander looked at him with an expression which Joe did not understand. But inside, Alexander was saying to himself, Joe, you ain't even a goddamn man, so how could you know? And then he relieved the tension in his cruel expression, and the tension around the table was relieved. He punched Joe playfully on his arm, and the men, like poker players after having diagnosed a bluff, relaxed and sipped their beer and smiled.

"Yeah, men, yeah," Joe said. This time he was complimenting himself. He had had two wives. Both of them had divorced him for mental cruelty. He shrugged this memory out of his mind, remembered that Alexander still held the floor, and said, "That's right, Lex. You're right."

Alexander felt good again. He had regained his prestige and their loyalty, and he had regained their attention without having to demand it. He thought he would play with them a while and tell them the story about the winter weekend he was lost in the bush in Timmins. But instead of telling them the truth — that he had cried like a child while his Indian woman left to go back to the camp for help — he decided to tell them it was *he* who had insisted she go back while he lay in the snow for forty-five hours with his right leg frozen like an igloo. And of course they believed him. When he told them the story, they nodded and patted him on his back with their smiles and with a free round of beer. Every man bought him a beer. Alexander never bought anybody a round.

"My Indian woman fell sick on the way back to the camp, so they had to leave her behind. At the camp. Then they went and lost their way, those bastards lost their goddamn way. Took the bastards five hours more than I figured it would take them to find me. OPP even sent in a helicopter. And there I was in the goddamn snow, my right foot feeling like a ton o' bricks, lifeless. And you know what? I'd just killed me a rabbit and was eating it raw when they arrived. And they said. . ."

"*A rabbit?*" Joe shouted, enjoying the story. "Hey, you hear that, fellas? A rabbit!"

The men were not the outdoor type. None of them had ever lived in the North. It was doubtful whether they knew the kind of animals to be found in the northern bush. But they laughed anyhow. It was a damn good story, they said. A damn fine story. And Alexander told it like a master, like a man, like a real man, which they all thought he was.

Now it was time to go home to his wife.

Alexander pushed his glass with some beer still in it, warm like plain tea, from in front of him. He made the first gesture to stand. And the others immediately scratched their chairs on the noisy sand on the floor and got up. They all began to talk about their wives being annoyed because supper had to be put into the oven to keep warm. But Joe, who wasn't married now, merely commented upon what an enjoyable Friday afternoon it had been listening to Lex. If it wasn't so late, and if they didn't have wives, and if they hadn't kept their wives waiting for supper and Friday-night shopping, he would invite Lex to return later in the evening and ask him to tell some more stories. But it was late now, they all agreed. Eight o'clock, and they hadn't gone home to their wives with their wages.

"If you fellas were *men*, you won't have to. . ." Alexander began, and he finished the rest of his opinion in a hoarse laugh filled with the pebbles of his deep voice and the bubbling suds of too much beer on an empty stomach.

"Yeah, yeah!" Joe chimed in. "Tell 'em, Lex, you tell

'em! If they was men. . . Christ, when I was a married man and my wife ever so much as opened her. . ."

Alexander scraped his heavy feet on the sand and straightened himself. "Well, men," he said, putting an Export into his mouth, "thanks for your company." Joe had raised his lighter to Lex's cigarette. "'Slong, fellas!!" He slapped each of them except Joe on his back, as he had done every evening when he was leaving, as he had seen army sergeants do on television. And then he left.

Joe caught up with him as he turned the corner to walk along Sherbourne, in the direction of the rooming houses with their dark foreboding hallways, where women sat on front steps with their blue-veined legs tucked into the crux of their cheap cotton dresses, white like their legs. Alexander hadn't looked back for Joe. And Joe, mumbling in his words and in his walk, the beer making rubber of his legs, was chipping along a step behind Lex, as if his feet were spades scraping the sidewalk.

"You really told 'em back there, Lex. You really socked it to 'em. I like that one 'bout the time you got lost. And they couldn't find you! And you stayed there, like a giant! Like a hero! Waiting for help. And all the time you was waiting, all the time you're waiting in that damn cold, you was there, cool as a goddamn cucumber. Eating a raw rabbit!" He laughed. He was coughing. He started again to laugh and cough. And then he was coughing and trying to laugh, and all the time he was saying, "A rabbit! Imagine that! A goddamn raw rabbit!" And he would splutter into a coughing and laughing fit and touch Lex with his elbow, trying to do all these things and still keep up with Alexander's pace. "A goddamn rabbit!" He spluttered some more. Saliva and stale beer touched his lips. He brushed it away with the back of his hand, and then he spat into the gutter. He nudged Lex with his elbow and said, "You know something, Lex? You wanna know something, old buddy?" Alexander continued walking, thinking of his wife waiting for him at home. "You know what, Lex? I wish I was like you. Really. No, really. I wish I was like you."

Something was bothering Alexander. But the way he walked, a little in front of Joe, made Joe think that he was worrying him, that Lex didn't want to talk anymore, that he was probably thinking about very important things. And Joe thought he was not deferential enough to Lex.

"Now don't get vex, Lex, old buddy. But I mean to say that, sitting down in that beer parlour, lis'ning to you talk the way you talked about the old days, it made me wish that my life was like your life, that I still had a woman at home, even a woman with a ring on her goddamn finger, even a wife, man! And I know that if I was just like you, I could be like you in that kind o' thing, having a wife, just like you have a wife. I know that I would be the boss in the house, that I won't make that mistake I make two times in the past and let her wear the goddamn pants. Not in my house. You understand me, Lex, buddy?"

Something wooden and staunch in Alexander's movement was now taking Joe's attention off what he wanted to say. Alexander seemed tense. He seemed to be angry that Joe was talking so much. To Joe it looked as if his steps were getting stiff. . .

It could have been the frostbitten leg tightening up, could have been the amount of beer he had drunk. But Lex can take his liquor, man. Lex can drink any man under the table! Nobody could take his liquor like Lex!

Alexander was moving away from him. And as Joe was thinking about Lex's rugged character, his man's rugged character, in that split second when his words and thoughts wrapped him inside Lex's skin and he was Lex, that moment of acclaim and idolization, that same moment of approval was when Alexander shifted his weight off his right leg, off the sidewalk, and was heading for his home, a desolate brown brick building with a woman past middle age sitting on the front steps looking at the cars and people going home along Sherbourne. The woman was sitting with her greying shanks propped up to show the blueness of veins around her knees.

Joe had never walked him home before, and didn't know he lived so close to the Selby Hotel. He had only sat with him and the other men in the dying light-bulbed room where you couldn't really see a man's face, where you didn't really know a man by complexion or features, both of which were dimmed in the light which the proprietor called "cozy." And Joe had never walked so close, so long, beside Lex before. But today he had been carried away by some of the things, some of the drama of the strong man's views contained in the story about the raw rabbit. Now he had dared to walk with Lex and confess that if no other man around the shining black table was impressed, he was.

Joe had come out of his dream of worship in time to see Alexander turn off the sidewalk and head for the woman sitting with her hands concealed in her lap.

The woman shifted her body ever so slightly. She was like a boxer moving her large hips over the cement of the steps to let Alexander pass.

Seeing his friend about to enter the house, Joe said, "Lex, I don't mean to bug you, but I hope you didn't mind me walking home with you like this, without you inviting me or anything, but I just want you to know that what you was telling me and the fellas back there in the beer parlour made a strange impression on me. I don't know how to say this, Lex, buddy, things like this I can't say too well, but I want to tell that you made me feel like a man today. You did. You make me feel, well, that's why I had to walk all the way over here with you, so that when you come to drink with the fellas tomorrow, even before you come, I want you to know you have a friend in me, and that I see a man in you, and that's why. . ."

The fat woman on the steps turned her bulky body around and said as if she was talking to the wind, "Ya better go in now before it's too late, son. She been. . ."

"Look, I gotta go in, Joe," Alexander said with an earnestness in his voice, a tinge of fear too, that Joe had never noticed before. "I wish we could talk now. You and me. As men. But maybe tomorrow, eh?" He looked scared. He would have said more but he knew he didn't have the time. He looked like a man giving a final important farewell. "Maybe tomorrow, eh? Tomorrow?"

At that moment they could hear the marching from down the dark hallway coming towards them. And the voice as if it was just then being released from the throat, soft at first with the distance and the darkness of the house, and finally screaming, and the woman, a thin piece of a stick of a woman, was saying, "I thought I told you last night! Last night I said, make it the last time. . ."

But she did not finish her threat. Instead, she came down the two steps at Alexander. Joe was standing stupidly beside him, not knowing what to do, not knowing if there was anything to do. The woman came at Alexander and shouted, *"Stannup!* Come, boy, stannup! *Stand up!"* in two distinct bullets.

And Alexander, Lex, the man who had waited so long in the snow, put his right hand dutifully on her shoulder while she bent down to his height.

She gripped his right leg. She pulled his trousers on that side of his body down, down, down, until it exposed a large canvas-type belt that sawmills use. And without another word she unbuckled some smaller belts and buckles. Alexander's heel struck the floor. Joe smelled sausages cooking inside.

With his hand still on the hardness of his wife's back, Alexander buried his face in the floor of linoleum, while the wife pulled the lifeless, eternally frostbitten and snow-devoured right leg out of the khaki trouser leg. Joe smelled the sausages inside and his eyes began to water. He was crying.

The woman sitting on the front steps did not even look back. She sat, and her relaxed fat back, flabby in the cotton dress, said that it had happened many times before.

Alexander's wife pulled the other trouser leg off. She kicked the wooden leg inside the dark hallway. And she said to Alexander, standing in his one-legged underpants, *"Move,* bugger! Move! Now!"* It was like four more bullets. Joe saw Lex stumble. Then he put out his right hand to touch the door post. And when he could feel the strength of the post, he lowered himself down to the floor, onto his hands. On one leg. In this posture he moved down into the further darkness of the dark house.

Joe did not want to see any more, and still he wanted to watch. He had turned his face away when Lex first bent down to reach the floor. And he was going to look back to see whether Lex resembled something, some animal he knew, something that Lex himself had talked about in any of his stories. But, instead, he walked back down the steps, past the woman watching the traffic along Sherbourne Street. She sensed when he was beside her, and without moving a muscle in her billowy body, she said, "Good night now."

The Discipline

...AND I REMEMBER, FROM THE TIME I COULD remember, seeing my grandmother go behind the velour curtain that separated her "room" from the rest of the house in which we all lived, father, mother, brother and me, punctually at eight o'clock each Saturday evening. The moment she closed the blind, the BBC overseas news came on. She disappeared from us for the rest of that night; and from behind the black curtain her words would join us as she mumbled verses from the Bible. . ."in the dark they dig through houses, which they had marked for themselves in the daytime." It seemed as if her voice was meant to discipline the rest of us. I grew up with this discipline.

And I remember her leaving the house at twenty-nine minutes to eleven each Sunday morning, in rain and in sunshine, dressed in a black sharkskin dress down to her ankles, her arms manacled by the white ruff, her neck ruffled also, and starched and ironed; black worn Bible in her right hand, a walking cane in her left, she'd go to matins at St. Barnabas Anglican Church.

And I remember her returning to the house at one, to the house now filled with the smells of Sunday dinner. I walked with her many times: as a boy, and even as a man. It took her a longer time to walk back. And on the way back, she would walk and stop, and talk and inquire about children and chickens and women in the family way, and men in hospital or overseas. She urged all the women, even those who were not mothers, to attend the Mothers' Union meeting at the church on Monday evenings. She would hold my hand during these Sunday journeys, for support, and then for love. . .

The office in which I am sitting now with this woman is in Toronto on Bay Street, on the fourteenth floor, in a building whose insides and offices have been renovated to make them look old and English, and financial. This office is stiff and panelled. The woman wears black, and she's as stiff as the ruffs on my grandmother's dress. She has just told me that her services will cost me one thousand dollars, "two hundred now, the rest in four equal instalments," to get me off the charge — "as a favour," she adds, using the same voice I had heard my grandmother use when she gave me a Kit-Kat chocolate. But unlike my grandmother, she said it like a curse. "I have to charge you this amount because the charge is a serious one."

Everything in this city is a charge. I am charged when I park my car in front of my house. I am charged to get permission from the city to park my car. I am charged again if I do not get permission from the city. I am charged and I am charged.

The car suddenly stopped working the day after I was last charged. . .

"I don't understand why you're telling me all this about the way your grandmother brought you up. We all had mothers and grandmothers." She said that as if it was a shame.

She lights a cigarette, swings her chair without making any noise. This office is so silent! It could be in Barbados in the small house at eight o'clock on any Saturday evening. She faces the buildings that look through the window at us, that show us the backs of women sitting at typewriters and moving behind screens; and all I have to talk to now is the silk middle of her black waistcoat. She is dressed like a man in a three-piece suit. The back of her head and the sweep of her hair make me feel her strength and her force, and I think of her as a man. Her muscles jerk each time I tell her something I remember. I'm giving her the evidence.

Without turning to face me, she says, "You're charged with assaulting your son."

"Assaulting my son?"

"You beat him up."

"I slapped him."

"You struck him with your fist. You smashed his ribs."

"I disciplined him."

"You didn't discipline him. You assaulted him."

"I disciplined him."

"You brutalized the boy. The crown will say you brutally assaulted him."

Her back is still turned to me.

. . .and I remember that I came home one day, the end of the month, with my salary from the Civil Service, inflated as my ego. And my grandmother made me sit down, and she counted the money and gave me my share. One-fifth. She handed my mother her share — she didn't mention my father! — and then she told me, "Because you're drawing a paycheque, it don't mean you is a man. You hear me?" And each payday she did the same thing, with the same regularity as her ritual of going to church. She met me at the door the next morning as I was leaving for work, and she told me, "You are still a child in this house. You will always be a child, no matter how old you get."

I remember I came home after twelve-thirty one night, even though I was twenty-eight years old, and she said, while my mother remained silent in her approval, "You is not the man in this house! You hear me? Your father, wherever the hell he is, is the *only* man here." She never gave me a key. The door was locked after that at eight o'clock each night.

I remember when I passed the Cambridge school-leaving certificate which qualified me to enter the Civil Service, I decided to leave her, to escape her discipline, to emigrate, to have a better life in Canada. The moment I entered the front door, my grandmother came up to me, and I thought she had come to congratulate me. But in her hand was an old shoe. It belonged to my father. She held the shoe, tapping it nervously against her long dress, not smiling, with my mother sombre beside her, she said, "Once a child, always a child." And then, with no warning of her change of attitude from anger to resignation, she broke into the hymn, one of her favourites, *Oh God, our help in ages past!* And when she could not remember the words, she improvised with *"always a child, always a child. . ."*

"Really! I don't understand why you're telling me all this," the woman lawyer said.

The large chair wheeled around and I was facing her neck, with a long linked gold chain around it and an oval watch attached. I thought I could hear it ticking. It was soft and appeasing and soothing, that magnificent small oval piece of ticking and tocking workmanship. It hung between her breasts. On the outside. And it rested in the softness of her white silk blouse that had long sleeves with ruffles on the wrist. I imagined the muscles beneath the soft silk. She held the golden oval, grabbed it really, and immediately became tense. I could see the time. "Twelve-thirty," she said as if she didn't want it to be so late. "You're living in the past. We need to know the present."

I was trying to make her see that the defence of my present predicament and the future was to be found in my ability to remember the past.

"Everybody has a past." She ran her hands through the thick files on her desk and gave them importance. She touched the bundles the way men ruffle through huge sums of money. There were only three files on the desk. All the other briefs and opinions of jurisprudence she had already committed and kept in her head. I looked at her head. It was a large, prominent head.

"Forget your past. In the present circumstances, talking about your *case*, I would suggest that you forget everything about your past. . ."

And I remember thinking of those days in Barbados, secure because I knew where I would end up when I crossed the threshold of a door and ventured into the bright mornings or the sensual evenings; and I knew who I would meet at the end of each street on each journey; I knew who to call a friend and who to ignore as enemy, and who to love. I remember how bold and cautionless I was, for there was no need for pretences; and I knew that when I died I would be protected on all sides of the brown polished box, in the warm, thick welcome of dust and ashes.

"Oh, by the way," she said, "please wear something dark, a conservative suit." I knew I was dismissed, although she did not say so.

I missed my stop after that. On the way from her office to Millicent Street where I live, where there was a bus stop beside the traffic lights two blocks before the street, I missed my stop.

In all the time I've lived in this neighbourhood of Italians, Portuguese, Indians from Pakistan and Canadians who leave for work before the sun rises, I have never been sure which stop is mine.

In the summer and the warm weather, when I can see better, when the afternoons are not cold, bare and white, and the road is not hazy as if covered by cigarette smoke and every house in the row looks alike, I can see for blocks and blocks in the almost West Indian road. And at six o'clock, behind the thick curtain like my grandmother's "room," I imagine I'm not in this cold, cramped, cruel country.

When I reach home, the lock on the front door is frozen. My hand is as frozen as the slit of the brass-coloured key. And when I put the key into the slit, I still have another key to put into the door. Two keys for one door. For this is a neighbourhood and a fortress of night latches and double locks, deadbolts and suspicion.

The children of this neighbourhood come out numerous as Dutch bulbs in the summer; as thick as weeds after a rainfall in Barbados. And none of these children ever said "Good morning" in a language I could understand. Some of them, boys mainly, I would find sitting on my new couch with their shoes melting, or running on my new carpet, bought on time from the Italian store where I paid more because I did not understand his English after he asked me if I had a language black people spoke. And my own son would be in their midst, eating popcorn and potato chips, speaking English like an Italian, and Italian too; and leaving the crumbs and destroying the pattern on the carpet.

My son is their age and equal in their language and customs. He can no longer understand the way I speak. And my discipline to him is the same as their language to me. With a new anger strange to me, and a new resentment each time I tell him the couch costs money, each time I tell him about my grandmother, he says, "I was born here."

My wife leaves at ten in the evening for the Toronto General Hospital, to work as a nurses' aide until seven or eight the next morning. Our lives overlap and crisscross and barely touch except for one day on weekends.

My son has again brought his friends into the empty

house. He has his key. He's a man. He cannot get into the house without his own key, for I get home from my cleaning job at five. Until four in the afternoon I run messages for the large firm on Bay Street where my woman lawyer works; and from nine at night and before they arrive the next morning, I clean their offices. My immediate boss, the manager, is a woman. Her boss is a woman, and the head of the firm is a woman. The only worker under me is another man from Jamaica.

I'm a man with a wife and a son thirteen years old and a house with two locks on the front door. And still I have to justify and explain to a woman who does not know me, and scarcely knows my ability to pay one thousand dollars in fees, that I have the right, as my grandmother had the right, to chastise a child; and that biblical blessing drove me to discipline him.

Yes, as a man I drove my hand across his face when he continued to disobey me. And the blow blew this profanity from his lips: "You're a damn old-fashioned West Indian. I was born here, man! I am a Canadian." He said that to me. The words flew from his lips, and the uncontrolled venom and spit struck me in the face, cold as I was always cold when I stood for minutes on the exposed front step, trying to open the two locks.

I was still cold when I recovered from the words of his new allegiance. *I am a Canadian* repeated itself like an echo, like a bad dream that you have more than twice in one night. In the dream he said, *You are dead and I am alive. I am alive but you are dead.* My right hand was driven to the nearest object. We were standing in the kitchen, feet apart, for when he said it, spit from his mouth touched me, we were so close. My hand lifted the chair, and I felt the impact of wood on flesh and the dis-integration of the chair in the rage and disappointment. . .

I did not sleep that night. I lay on my back in thought;

and when the thoughts weakened, I heard the breathing beside me and the murmuring of speculation and hope. My wife had just come to bed. "That would teach him. Canadian children don't have any damn discipline." She pronounced the word *dis-cip-pline.* "I see some o' them where I works talking back to their mothers in front o' strangers, making the poor mothers 'shame-'shame-'shame, and even I myself have to turn my head aside, I does be so 'shame too!"

The boy had said nothing. He didn't say another word about being a Canadian. I had made dinner for the two of us, which I did on Mondays, Tuesdays, Wednesdays, Thursdays and Fridays. And he sat on the same couch that had caused the problem, and I on the chesterfield, and together we watched television in silent disinterest until ten o'clock when he got up and left the room.

"I pay the 'lectric'ty and the taxes, as you ask me," she said, making an inventory of her own thoughts. "I wish we could go home for Christmas. What I won't give for a sea-bath!"

The moment he had left I felt very old and alone. I had tried to read the anger in his face while he was still sitting there, to see if it held such ugly disregard for me; whether throughout the long cowboy movie he had refused to look at me because we were really strangers already at war. I had tried to read his breathing and his disposition each time he changed the position of his elbow, or when he stretched his legs out and drew them in again, with each firing of the cowboy's gun. But he remained quiet. Once I even forgot that he was in the same room with me. "You know what I would like right now?" my wife was saying. "I could eat a flying fish with a dog!" I could not see exactly where the blow from the chair had landed, but I imagined it had struck him somewhere between his armpit and waist. His height and my own against his made that the likely spot. The tiresome voice of the woman beside me went on about flying fish and seabaths. . .

The next morning he said, "I'm going swimming." The city had recently opened a swimming pool and he and the neighbourhood children went there almost every day after school. I knew he could not swim, I thought I knew he could not swim, so I wished he would drown, and then I wished he would not drown.

A week passed. My son came and went. There were no crumbs and footprints on the carpet and couch. But one afternoon I saw footprints of different sizes on the bathroom floor, along the hall and right up to the front door. My son and his friends probably had not come at all. I couldn't think he would again disobey my orders, even though I began to feel that a mark on a couch or carpet was such a small thing to lose my temper over. So these footprints on the imitation marble floor of the bathroom, and along the linoleum of the hall to the front door, could have been my own or my wife's or his, or my dream or my thoughts. They could have been my wish for his disobedience so I could punish him.

He did not drown. And on the weekend he was still with us, and my wife was lying on her stomach beside me, lying on my back. I always lie on my back. The calypso music on the radio was soft. I was remembering my life back home, and comparing that life with this house full of furniture and electric kettles and electric blenders, equipment invented to make life easier. Cobwebs were in two corners on the ceiling. The left corner and the right corner. She turned over and noticed them and explained, "With all the things this place have to offer, don't you know I have never find a cobweb broom to buy!"

"Northamerica have all the opportunities a man could ask for, girl. . ."

The calypso was one we knew and had danced to; and

we listened, her leg on mine, between my legs, hands around my neck in a Boston-crab of rough passionate love.

"The boy in? Go and look in his room and see if that hard-ears boy get home yet. Northamerica have everything but dis-cip-pline. . ."

I remember my wife talking as if she was dreaming, prescribing a life for her child in this city she never grew to like or understand. On the one night we were home together long enough to be together, she spent all her time repeating this Epiphany. That was on the Saturday night after the calypso program on CHIN-FM had ended.

Now in all this time, remembering and relating my personal evidence to the woman in the law office, and remembering the incident with my son, I am still just inside the door with the two locks, standing on the linoleum, leaning against the wall that separates my house from the one through which I can hear music and heavy footsteps all hours of the night and day. I am hearing the music now. And I imagine that I can smell curry. Footsteps go up and come down; and as they come down, they seem heavier. . .

I took off my winter coat and started to think of the dark suit she told me to wear in the morning at ten o'clock. And I think about asking the woman, my immediate boss, for time off; and my bank manager, Mrs. Janet White, for a loan; and Miss Elizabeth Campbell at the mortgage company for a little more time. I was thinking about how I would have to approach all these powerful women in my life for help and sympathy. I thought, too, of my grandmother as I began to think of all these women controlling my life. My thoughts were as hands clinging to my grandmother's long black dress when she moved over the rocks and fallen tree branches on the path to church.

I remember when I got out of bed and went downstairs and walked along this same hallway where I'm standing now, counting all these women I must approach for mercy. Just as I reached the bottom of the stairs to look into his room, I heard the neighbours' curried music coming through the wall, as if the mallets that struck the drum had pierced its skin.

It was eight o'clock.

My wife had just got home. I was late leaving for work.

I passed over the noisy, cracked linoleum, opened the inside door to look through the peephole into the outside door with its two locks, when I saw the disfigured faces and eyes and large noses.

Through the peephole my vision of the faces was like a photograph held too close to the nose. I saw the shining buttons and the shining belt and the eyes that looked like glass; and I worked my eye down to the bottom of the hole to make the hole larger, to show me more focus to this disjointed watery picture. And it was at the bottom rim of the hole, like an eye filled with water, that I realized I was looking into the eyes of my own son.

"Pearl! Pearl!"

She came down, like the heavy bass drum next door, dressed in white Oxford shoes, pink panties, and with her pink uniform ripped from the neck down to the bottom of her belly, as if she was giving rapid, violent birth. The zipper had stopped five inches from the bottom of the dress. My two screams had caught her in this Caesarean act.

I remember the police officer coming in, after showing the boy inside, and after the young Canadian woman had entered. The police officer closed the door, and I felt my living room turn into a cell. It was the first time I was so close to a policeman. I smelled the serge and the leather and the polish of his uniform. And I saw the butt of his gun. I thought I smelled brass.

My wife sat with one hand to her mouth and the other closing the unzipped uniform. The policeman stood at attention beside my son, beside the Canadian woman.

I remember the policeman with his eyes riveted to the carpet. The Canadian woman looked around the room. Through the hallway door. Seeing things she wanted to memorize. I saw her blue eyes flick over two charcoal pictures. The Rasta man and the Rasta woman. I remember my son standing between the policeman and the woman. He looked calm, protected and distant. He looked as if he had chosen new parents. A new allegiance grew amongst the three of them. I remember hearing all the words the Canadian woman spoke. She used a calm, unpointed, objective monotone. She was talking about persons I had never met. But all the time, she was talking about me and my wife and the boy. I tried to follow each word, but I couldn't understand the language she used. The meaning of her words was above my head. She was speaking in English but her words came from books. She must have read these books many times and had memorized their texts.

"As his teacher, I cannot minimize the moral responsibility I have towards the social development of this boy, and even though he may have parents of his own, in a nuclear sense, I would be remiss in my responsibility if I didn't take it upon myself to take this action and seek to protect this boy, with the help of the authorities, from the environment in which, through no fault of his own, he now finds himself, and. . ."

In all this remembering time, I am still no farther inside my house than the few feet behind the front door with the two locks. From that morning when the policeman came with the summons charging me with the criminal offence of assault to cause bodily harm towards my own son, I have been walking in a dream of frightened thoughts. I read the *Star* to see if any other father has been found guilty of this offence, to find the sentence imposed on those fathers. And when I find it, I feel lost. I find myself walking up and down at work, at home, in the kitchen as I make dinner, in front of the house, in the cold whitened garden where all the roses and flowers I've planted have now become stiff brown pieces of stick. And each time I'm inside the house, I find myself turning the pages of the Bible to the Book of Psalms, just as my grandmother had been driven to her gold-leafed Bible to search for a verse to soothe the thorns of her life and problems. But I'm not seeing the words or the blurred wisdom of those words, for they are the same as the counselling the young Canadian woman had given me. . .

"Your Honour, I have been the boy's teacher in grade seven, grade eight and grade nine. His reading disability was the first clue to more basic problems in the home. Lack of security and so on. When I asked the boy to read 'My father is at work,' he would read 'My father gone from home.' This invention in perception led me to investigate the assault. I noticed that his attention span was getting very short, indeed. We care for all our children. So I called in the police and the authorities of the Children's Aid Society in order to protect this boy."

"Thank you, Miss Barron."

"And begging your pardon, Your Honour, if I may add one more point. The boy was an active participant before this happened. He has a healthy socialization tendency. Only after the problem I mentioned did I discover that his jaw was broken and. . ."

"Thank you."

"I examined the boy two days later. I found lacerations to his left side. Between the second and fifth ribs. In my estimation, the blow was caused by a sharp object. From close range."

"Could this blow or these blows have been delivered by a human hand? A fist, doctor?"

"A savage fist, Your Honour."

My wife was wearing black. I did not tell her to accompany me in this colour of the funeral, but she wore black because she wanted to look like a "good mother." She was sitting about ten seats away from me. I saw her raise her neck. And I saw her eyes fall on my hands. "Your Honour" had just mentioned "a human hand." My hands were in my lap, one covering the other.

The room was large and bright. There was a photograph of Queen Elizabeth II. Something like a coat of arms or a seal, complicated in its intricate design and workmanship, was on the wall. Out of the jumble of colours, white, blue, red and green, I could distinguish only an animal. A lion. There was another animal too. It had one horn. I had never seen one of these before, and I didn't know its name. Words were at the bottom of the seal, in a foreign language. I could read only the "mal" in this message. I did not know what it meant.

The room was panelled. It was quiet even when they were talking. There was a Canadian flag on the wall. A police officer stood beside me, outside the wooden dock. They had put a chair for me to sit on. I was the only person in this dock. Every now and then the men and the woman lawyer who represented me would say something in whispers. They were all smiling. I felt they all liked me because they smiled each time they looked at me. I smiled too.

A man who called himself The Crown said, "This vicious disregard for civilized practice and the principles of this country." He looked at me, then he looked at the jury. Then pointing at me without looking at me, as if he knew where I was, that I would not run from the dock, he said, "You have heard the evidence. . ."

The judge, Your Honour, sitting above us, dressed in black with some purple in his uniform, whispered something to my lawyer in Latin, then he looked at me and looked at my son who was sitting across from me in the same row without a wooden dock to protect him. It was as if he and I were in argument, as if he was put there to debate against me, just as I had seen people on television sit, pro and con, professional-man and con-man; or in the legislature down on Queen's Park, where big men in three-piece suits argue among themselves across a floor of thick carpet.

The minister of my church, the St. Clair Baptist Church, a Jamaican immigrant, had come, he and four "sisters" from the congregation, and were sitting on my left. Each time the man who called himself The Crown said "this vicious disregard," and each time the black-and-purple uniformed judge spoke, I looked to make sure they were still there, the minister with his highly polished mahogany skin and the four "sisters," and my wife dressed in black as if she was attending my grandmother's funeral. The six of them held down their heads as if they were ashamed of me each time The Crown repeated "this vicious disregard."

Another Canadian woman was now speaking. She wore spectacles with plastic frames. Her hair was thin and long and blonde. It was the same colour as her spectacles. The make-up on her lips and cheeks was red. When she spoke, the red lipstick became her words, wide, round, sharp, high and violent. "I have seen many cases of assault in my fifteen years as a social worker at the Children's Aid. And I can say that never, *but never,* have I seen a case as violent and brutal as this one. I have known many coloured immigrants. I sympathize with their problems. I understand they have to adjust to our way of life. And to our way of doing things. To our civilization and our society. But never, never, *but never,* in my fifteen years have I seen. . ."

I looked up in time to see her take a piece of pink tissue from her purse. She applied the pink tissue to her eyes, then her mouth. She looked now like a woman catching her breath, lost by a sudden punch in the ribs.

"I've made two trips to the West Indies, to Jamaica. For a firsthand, on-the-spot study of the cultural and social derivation of West Indians living here. My conclusion is that what we in the profession refer to as the predisposition for cultural violence among West Indian parents has its origins in the harsh historical background of slavery."

When she said that, my black suit tightened around me. The dock was now a vial. I became a specimen inside that vial. I could feel the sweat under my armpits. I became embarrassed that I smelled. I could not remember if in the rushed order of dressing I had rubbed the penis-shaped bottle of Right Guard over the thick black hairs under my arms. I was sweating. The room was cold but I was hot.

The Baptist minister and the four sisters shifted on the long wooden bench. My wife stirred too. I knew she stirred because I know that noise, that special ruffle of her shiny silk dress. I knew she moved the same instant I became hot.

I jumped up.

I saw my grandmother. I saw my mother. I saw the clean little house. I saw the whiteness of the sun on the road brutalizing it at the hottest time of the afternoon. The round clock on the wall said eleven. I saw myself on that warm road. And then I saw myself painted in their words, in the dock, by this brittle lady.

"No-oooooo!"

My lawyer in a black tailored suit, with her gold chain catching the light, got up from her chair and tried to cut me off; and then in a quick movement she apologized to The Crown and to "Your Honour" in case I said too much to make it bad for her and for myself.

"No!"

"Take the accused away."

It was the man in the black and purple, Your Honour, as they called him, who said it. He used a voice that was the same as if he had said, "Take the cream away." He must have used those four words many times. There was no emotion, no passion and no feeling in his manner. I thought he would have at least turned red, become angry and used the same anger in his words to match the faint protest in mine, or even to match my passion. I wanted to remind him that I was this boy's father, and as his father, I could discipline him. My grandmother had disciplined me.

The court was silent now. My word of objection had cut the tongues of the court's sanctity and whispering dignity.

"Take the accused away."

I was a dried fallen leaf that had to be raked away to keep the lawn pleasant and clean. Or a piece of banana skin kicked out of the way with a well-timed movement of the foot, to remove its slight danger from the path of law-abiding pedestrians who take cleanliness and safety for granted.

The police officer came into the wooden dock. With a sharp, short, practised click, he snapped the handcuffs on. With an equally practised push, I was on my feet and moving down to the basement cells, as if I had been released through a trapdoor.

As I was going down, they were still saying things about me.

"This is his first offence, yes, sir."

"He is at present employed."

"Checking with his neighbours, we learn that he stands in his garden talking to the flowers."

"I would recommend a light sentence, under the circumstances, Your Honour."

"They must be taught a lesson, that they're not back in the West Indies."

"I recommend a psychiatric examination."

I don't know where I am. I don't know who I am. All I know is that I'm alive. I'm on a white bed, a bed with white sheets and a white pillow. And I'm wearing white pyjamas. I'm happy, and sometimes I feel like a child, like the little boy I was in Barbados when my mother would say, "Boy, you hungry? You hungry, ain't you?" And she would feed me, and I would smile and eat whatever she gave me. It is like this, in this large room, with many small beds, all the same size, the same cleanliness, the same white walls with no pictures or photographs on them; and the bright clean light from the fluorescent bulbs. A woman with hair that is strong and looks like bright steel comes every morning since I've been here. She's dressed in a rich brown suit and brown shoes that shine. She asks me questions, and I give her answers by nodding my head and smiling.

"You feel lonely in this place, don't you?"

I nod.

"You hate this place, don't you?"

I nod.

"You don't think very much of our system, do you?"

I nod.

"The system has done you harm, hasn't it?"

I nod.

"And you would do anything, anything at all, to get back at the system, wouldn't you?"

I nod.

"Even destroy it?"

I nod.

"You're paranoid. Don't you feel paranoid?"

I nod.

"You're a violent man. You resort to violence to settle things which you can't settle with words, don't you?"

I like to nod my head. I nod nicely and properly, so she won't be annoyed with me. I like to make her happy. Each time I answer, she smiles and looks very happy and writes something in her book. And she smiles with me after she's written these things in her small, black-bound book. I smile and she smiles some more.

144

"Now, let me ask you a serious question, may I?"

I nod.

"If your son left potato chips on the couch or on the carpet again, would you knock him down? You would knock him down again with your fist, wouldn't you?"

I nod.

"If he came home later than ten o'clock on weekends, after you told him to get home by eight, you'd hit him with a chair again?"

I nod.

"And even break four or five or six ribs, more than the first time?"

I nod.

I like this small lady with the steel-grey hair and brown suit and shiny brown shoes. She reminds me of my grandmother.

One morning she brought me a chocolate bar. It was a Kit-Kat. My grandmother bought me a Kit-Kat chocolate bar every other Saturday when she went into town. I used to suck off all the chocolate until the bar became the colour of bone, and then squeeze the rest of the bar between my tongue and the roof of my mouth until it disappeared. It lasted longer that way.

"If you had your way, if you had it in your power, you'd do something to the teacher, wouldn't you? You don't like her or the lady from the Children's Aid Society or the entire legal system, do you?"

I nod.

And it went on like this, these happy mornings with the lady in the brown suit who'd come and ask me these questions. And I'd nod my head all the time because I wanted her to like me and feel I was a God-fearing, obedient man. I wanted her to feel that I myself was obedient as a little boy, just as I wanted her and all the others to feel that my own boy should be obedient.

And then one morning she didn't come.

When I was tired of waiting for her and was about to drop off into a doze, they awoke me and told me to dress in my black suit, that I was going back.

They made me think I was going back home.

When I got back, I would clean up my garden and paint the front door black and take off one of the locks because it was getting warmer now and I wouldn't freeze my fingers to the bone trying to find two slits in the door. And I was going to see the minister and thank him for losing two days' work by coming to court. And I would see my wife again, and we'd lie on the bed on Sunday nights and listen to calypso music and look at the ceiling to see if the two cobwebs were still there. And I could write to my mother and tell her that if God spare life, we'll be coming home for Christmas with the boy. She has never seen the boy.

And I would call my employer and tell her I'm sorry but this nice lady in the brown suit was asking me a lot of questions and I wanted to be nice to her; and since there were so many questions, I had to skip work longer than I expected. . .

But they put me in the back of a yellow panel truck, locked from the outside. It had chicken wire and bars at the top of the back door. Through this I saw people disappearing from me, getting smaller, Chinese and Japanese in size; and even those walking with their faces towards me were going backwards. They were all cut into small pieces by the mesh and iron on the door. Travelling backwards like this, I was soon between tall buildings and then underground. I could smell the fumes and the dust of parked cars and moving cars, all of which came through the chicken fence. I started to hear music.

It was loud music. Music from my part of the world. Did the neighbours who cooked curry and others know I was in this yellow panel truck? Underneath the heavy, stubborn and fatal beat, a beat like the determination of tribal drums — heavy wooden gavels on thick animal skin, and iron on iron — I heard these words: *Yuh running and yuh running and yuh running away. . . Yuh can't run away from yourself. . . Must-have-done, must-have-done something wrong. . .* I was in a dream. I was in an elevator. The light around me became better. I was now standing between two police officers. I wished the lady in the brown suit was with us.

The two police officers did not speak with me; and in the elevator they looked up and down, reading the numbers of the floors to themselves; and there was only the humming, the soft murmuring of strained muscles in the contraption that made the elevator rise with our weight.

I was back in court. When I entered, all conversation was cut short and heads turned in my direction.

The words of the underground song, *Yuh running and yuh running and yuh running*, and the gavel beating on heavy skin and the striking of iron on iron were running through my mind, and I began to feel the peace in the soft questioning voice of the lady in the brown suit.

The man dressed in black and purple began to speak. It was a soft voice, a voice I felt contained no feeling and no sympathy; a voice that I had now become used to hearing, even when people said the worst things about you, when people made decisions that sent you unemployed through a winter, when they said things that did not help you understand that your telephone had been cut off, that your heat had been stopped. . .

". . . in view of the psychiatrist's report, it is the opinion of the court that the defendant shows a tendency. . ."

He must have been talking for some time, for I could see my lawyer lean back, sit up, shift in her seat, adjust to the ceremony of words.

And then it was over. It was over without a stir. It was over without confusion. In this room with no wind blowing, with the temperature even at the breathing point, with no coughing or clearing of the throat, in this court with the same sacred stillness of the front pews in that church in Barbados, it was over. The last words that I heard from the man on the raised seat, Your Honour, were "Five months. . ."

Five months. *Yuh running and yuh running and yuh running away*. . . And the lady in the brown suit who had been so understanding in her questions passed before me in a swift brown blur. And then my lawyer came over and rested her hand on my shoulder. I could not even feel the weight of her heavy acknowledgement. Her perfume was like the Kit-Kat chocolate bar. She was looking above my head, not into my eyes; and just as I looked around to see if there was someone behind me, I saw my son walking between my wife and the Canadian teacher.

The oval watch on the heavy chain was uneven around my lawyer's neck and it shone like a large teardrop. Her hand felt heavier now. The heaviness of the hand became the total weight of my body.

"Do you have anything to say to me?" She seemed to be in a hurry. Perhaps she had another man to defend.

I shook my head.

"Good!"

I nodded.

"If you'd like me to talk to the judge and tell him what you've been telling me about your grandmother. . ."

I shook my head.

"Good! Because you've already been sentenced."

"Can I talk now?"

"You can't talk now."

All the way back out, into the past of dust and the fumes and the mysterious music with its heavy gavel on thick skin, travelling over the details of the previous journey, small people walking backwards, their faces punctuated and cut up into pieces through the perspective of the chicken wire and bars, I was now sitting between two new police officers. They were protected from me. Both my hands were tied behind my back with handcuffs. I could not stand up to face the former journey and see the progress of the curving steel of the streetcar tracks, or the potholes in the city streets, or the hairpin bends I was now taking. The yellow panel truck slid off the parallel steel lines and forced me against one of the two police officers who twinned me in the locked embracing manacles. His hand touched mine to keep me upright and from falling on my face; and the force of that touch jerked my recollection to that path through fields of sugar canes and hedges of guinea grass and peas, winding like this road, more voluntary but disciplined, in the firm grasp of my grandmother's sticky hand as we walked that last mile to face the church.

A Slow Death

IT BEGAN VERY SLOWLY, ALMOST IMPERCEPTIBLY, his hating the house in which he lived for fifteen years; and without warning, like the melting of the stub of snow at the end of his walk that signalled in the spring. This hatred became a rage, an explosion, and consumed his mind. It happened soon after his wife died. Her scent and her spirit remained in the house, quiet at first, and like an aggressive tenant afterwards, taking up most of his time and his space, although he was now occupying the three-storied house by himself.

He told the young, vivacious saleswoman that he had to sell the house because it had become too large for him. He did not tell her about his wife.

He showed her through the house, on the three floors of rooms which he had recently cleaned and painted. Linoleum was nailed down the very morning it was bought from Bloor Hardware. The heads of the nails were still shining and visible. When he took her into the bathroom, the fresh, high, pungent smell of the small white balls he had taken from the storeroom at work returned his wife's smell, the smell of camphor.

He had mourned for three weeks, with the help of Canadian Club rye whisky. And he would have mourned longer if the rye had sat less heavily upon him, and hadn't made him drop off in dozes in the middle of the day, and hadn't built up a pallor of ennui around his entire personality. He felt tired all the time. Cigarettes and more rye did not help.

He became suddenly tired, almost exhausted, by climbing the three flights of stairs. He began to hate her and her gnawing memory each time he got drunk. And he was drunk these days more often than the evenings of the weekend, which had been his time for relaxation and the occasional drink.

The saleswoman smiled all the time. He could not guess at her seriousness or interest in his home. But at the end of the showing, she said, "I'll take it off your hands." He did not like the way she said it. He did not like the way she was dressed. During the interview she had pulled the tape measure from the neck of her cashmere sweater, like a snake unfolding, dropped it in one corner of the bedroom, after having kicked aside a shoe box, and then she bent down without bending her knees so that the ridge of her behind faced him as she certified the size of the room. It was in the bedroom in which his wife had died that she bent down this way for the first time. He was still aware of his wife's presence in the room.

Whenever he saw her legs and the colour of her panties, he turned his eyes away. But he had taken a full appraisal of her young body and sensual legs; and his age told him he could be her father, and therefore he had probably called the wrong real estate company. She said her name was Jennie Cambull. But she was pretty. He tried to see a comparison between her and his wife, but he could not remember when his wife looked as young as this self-assured woman in the transparent dress. The shoe box she had kicked aside contained his wife's jewels.

Nevertheless, he signed the agreement to sell. "I'll take

it off your hands," she said again, and then left.

On the subway going back to work in the east end, he was sad. He had agreed to sign his life away, and would probably be lonely and desolate and would have to enter a home for the aged. He wished he had had children. He would happily live in one room and give the children the run of the rest of the house. He wished the city would transfer him to the park across the street from his house. From his house to the city park where he worked as a gardener, down in the Beaches, was a daily journey of almost one hour by streetcar. At five o'clock it took almost twice as long. But the time spent travelling whetted his thirst for rye, and it also kept him away from the house.

Many nights soon after she died, he would walk up and down the house, talking to her, which he never did when she was alive, re-arranging her clothes and playing with her jewels in the shoe box.

The weekend was upon him. It was Friday afternoon. As he got off the streetcar near the race course at Greenwood, a clock on a large brick building said two. He would have the weekend to himself, all of Friday night, all Saturday and Sunday, but he could not face another weekend alone in the house that seemed filled with echoes of a past, unhappy life. He had already done all those small jobs that old men occupy their hands with, leaving their minds to wander and be oppressed by loneliness and advancing helplessness. He had always feared, even when he was fifty, that he would have a hard time going to the toilet and that there would be no one to clean him afterwards. This was one reason he hated her for dying before he did. And now all he had to look forward to were the rough hands of an indifferent, unrelated public nurse in a home for the aged. But that was better than living in this large house alone, to be lathered in his own excrement and be found dead. He wondered if the smell of his excrement would be the same he would give off when he was found dead. This Friday evening he stifled these thoughts with a half bottle of Canadian Club.

He had chosen this house because of the park. The park and the price of the house. He had lived for ten years in a rooming house opposite; and when the For Sale sign was nailed into the snow in mid-February, he saw it early. That afternoon he was walking through the park. Sibelius Park was as lovely and boisterous with snow and children's laughter as was the music of the composer after whom the park was named. He had saved three thousand dollars in ten years. Once a month, on each payday, with a constancy that matched his wife's attendance at the Shaw Street Baptist Church, he went to his bank to make his deposit. This regularity impressed the bank manager. When the time came for purchase and a loan, the bank manager gave him the extra three thousand dollars to make the down payment. "You're a steady man," he told him. The price was twenty-five thousand dollars.

When he came home that night, he announced his good fortune to his wife. He was the first in both their families to own the roof over their heads. He poured himself a rye and ginger, and poured one for his wife. And together they stood at the window of their flat on the third floor of the rooming house and looked across at their new home. He dreamed of improvements and flower beds and green-painted fences and red roses and new linoleum.

He faced the new life before him — new, but only as large as the width of the quiet dog-deserted street — with the same bravery as he had faced the steps of the Air Canada plane that brought him here from Barbados twenty-five years ago.

Fifteen years ago this house was on a street whose houses had an ordinary beauty and working-class charm. The street was inhabited by Jews and Anglo-Saxons who were still trampling through snow to catch a five-o'clock streetcar in the morning; by people of modest means and fair-sized families, with children who played safely in the park. But all of a sudden the street became popular, enviable and expensive; and just as suddenly the neighbourhood became known as The Annex. He never found out what it was annexed to. But the droves of refugees from the suburbs and from Europe's poorest countries transformed it into a village.

"Town-housing" sprang up like the bulbs he nurtured in the city parks. He watched the street change from a stable, working-class district to one made up of lawyers, university professors and architects. They filled the sidewalks in front of his house and his shared laneway with the guts of their renovations. Dust and brick and broken plaster lay for days beside the demolished front lawns. And in the racket of the improvements, he remained silent and disapproving, suffering from long bouts of sinus caused by the dust of regenerated homes.

The owners, wallowing in new money, delighted in destroying the old gracious charm of these houses bought by the sweat and blood of ambition; and they resold them after one year for small fortunes, and the street became infested with transients who bought and sold and had no time for families and for sitting amongst the flowers and the playing children and the barking dogs in the park.

The first thing he did when he moved into his home was turn the volume of his Seabreeze record player up as loudly as it would go. He stood with a broad smile on his face, laughing with his wife who covered her ears with her hands, and he cried out, "I am now a man!" She shrugged and moved away, but there was a smile on her face.

He experienced new privacy. He used the bathroom with the door wide open, and the sound of his passing gas went from the second floor to the first where she was washing the dinner plates. "Ahhh! I wanted to do that for ten years! Excuse me."

As the years passed, he loved the park more and it became a vacationland of his imagination. In winter the crystals of leaves and icicles shone white and splendid, and he sat by his bay window and watched this magic, helped on by the strength of his rye and ginger ale.

In the spring, which it is now, he counted the erupting new life of plants and flowers, Dutch bulbs and green grass around him; and at his job in the east end, he wallowed in these new shoots of life and felt himself getting younger. Every year at this time, and for years now, he pestered his supervisor for a transfer. "Everything takes time," his wife would say, but it only made him more impatient and angry with her. "A man like me, used to watching and waiting on bulbs and plants and things to grow, and that is *all* you could say?" She did not understand him, did not understand his anger, his ambition for their success, his ambition to be his own man.

On this Friday night, as on every Friday night since she had died, he did the shopping for the groceries and topped off the plastic bag that had a large red D with two forty-ounce bottles of Canadian Club. He already had a case of ginger ale in the cupboard beneath the sink. He took a shower and put on a green long-sleeved shirt and green trousers, the same as the uniform he had to wear to work. *City* was stitched in large letters on his left-hand breast pocket. He threw the uniform which he had worn during the week, and which fitted him no better than the fresh one, into the dirty-clothes hamper. He did not close the lid.

After the news and the first television movie, after five drinks, he still faced a long night. So he got up from his favourite leather chair that grew higher and longer when he sat upon it at a certain angle, and embarked on his nightly roaming through the house. He touched the backs of chairs and ran his calloused hands over the crocheted antimacassars on the heavy upholstered furniture. Grease was left on them. He went to the third floor in the voiceless house, to the room where he'd been sleeping since she died, and took out the ten suits he owned. He had bought the material cheap in the garment district on Spadina Avenue and had given it to a West Indian tailor. The suits were all of wool, made in the same style, and with waistcoats. He never wore nine of them; and the one that touched his back was worn only once. But every Sunday morning, in the spring and in the summer, he put them on the pink plastic clotheslines in his backyard to get the sun and the air. Mothballs were in all the pockets of each suit. And in the lapel of the black serge suit was the white carnation, dried and dead now, which he had worn to his wife's funeral.

He sat on the bed, with five suits on each side, and ran his thick birthmarked palms delicately over the rich material. He smiled as he discovered the tailor's bill in the breast pocket of one of them, the subway transfer ticket in the waistcoat of another; and these two mementos did not bring back any clues to a life that seemed to have ended long ago. He replaced the bill and the transfer ticket.

Even when she was alive he delighted in these expeditions. His delight was no less this Friday evening. He used to put his father's suits on the line to sun when he was a boy. His father had two suits, a black one for funerals and church, a dark-brown one for weddings and "service-of-songs" and dances, which were called "balls" in those days.

"Any cockfight," he said, as if he was talking to his wife, and as he had joked with her each Sunday morning before she left for church as he prepared his suits for airing, "any cockfight, and I can't be caught with my pants down! I prepared for any cockfight. Funeral or wedding."

He didn't know that the funeral would be his wife's.

Even now he wondered whether he hadn't, by his harmless words, brought on her death. She had taken ill on a Wednesday, called the doctor on a Friday, and the following Thursday she was dead. It was cancer. She had borne it silently for one year before she confessed her pains to the doctor. Cancer.

But he must not think of her long, silent suffering and swift departure now. The house was still in mourning.

At the bottom of the clothes closet from which he had taken the ten suits was a line of shoes, black and brown, stiff from lack of wearing, and shining bright from the weekly polishing he gave them. They were perforated at the instep, and they all had rubber heels. He hated noise. These he took out, all twelve pairs, and as he had seen his father do every Sunday morning, he polished them with Nugget, black and brown, and spat on them twenty-four times to improve their shine.

He's in the bedroom where she died. He brushes the dust from her large black Bible. He rests his hand on its cover, like a man swearing to tell the truth, and for the first time he has a strong urge to open the Bible. The pages, trimmed in gold, fall apart, dividing the book almost in half, and he sees the lines: *The sleep of the labouring man is sweet, whether he eat little or much: but the abundance of the rich will not suffer him to sleep.* Was she trying to tell him something? It could not have been an accident that his eyes would fall upon this passage. The pages had fallen open on their own when he held the Bible. It was as if the Bible had reorganized its weight to be balanced in two almost equal halves.

He began to remember how her voice wheezed when she read. A soft, almost bronchial whispering. And then he noticed the smell of her bathwater, Bournes Bay Rum. It was the smell of death too, that same smell he had noticed in the funeral parlour. And although his friends from the city parks department had sent fresh flowers and wreaths that took up one entire pew, her smell, body and bathwater, was stronger.

What is the time now? The bottle is less than half empty. He looks out onto his former landlady's house. He knows her profession because he knows her, and they say good morning to each other. But the men and women and children in all the other houses have remained strangers. He does not see them except on weekends. His hours are not theirs. And no one except his former landlady has ever come to ask how he is now that he's alone. Perhaps they do not even know he's alone. Perhaps they do not even know she's died. At home in Barbados the coffin and the service would be in the front room, and the whole village would know and would mourn. But her body was placed in the balmed safekeeping of a funeral home. Out of sight, out of memory. Could he die in this house and nobody would know until the gas company came to read the metre?

The street is quiet and ordinary. There's only the normal activity of people passing. No one pauses, no one's aware of him, no one looks up and sees anything different. Their lives have not changed. A woman passes with a plastic bag of groceries. A foreign car stops, turns off its lights, and the driver locks the door and disappears in the larger darkness. That's the man who wears a beard and walks with books in both hands. The woman with the plastic bag enters the house beside his through a heavy black door that has brass rectangles on it. Perhaps she's a lawyer.

Three Indians pass. One of them drops the bag from which he's eating. He casts his eyes right and left, above and behind, then digs his left hand deep into the seat of his trousers, shivers and walks on. He laughs. Perhaps his companions have seen him in the shadows at the second-floor curtain. They're all wearing cloth wrapped around their heads, and the street light turns the cloth into shimmering silver.

He had never seen them on this street before. He wondered where they were born. He was glad they did not live on the street.

How much more could he bear?

He does not watch much television, even though he turns it on every night, for there's too much crime and murder coming into his living room. Last week a nine-year-old girl was missing from the park; and after searching for her for two days, they found her cold in an unused refrigerator, strangled and raped and buckled into two, like a flying fish, to suit the size of her attacker's whim. The refrigerator was still plugged into the wall. Every week in the Toronto *Star* you read that a man killed a man or a woman, and sometimes two or three; and on television you see thousands killed or starving to death. In Africa, which he doesn't know and doesn't care to see but which he hears a lot about, the television shows him images of ribs and dried flesh, and flies on black faces. And before the story ends — the suffering on the faces or the images on the screen — he shuts it out and turns it off.

But there was one night when he could have borne more. That was the night, many years ago, which he relives even now. The smell of meat in old oil had disappeared. The house was still. Rose and pine, the smells his former landlady favoured and kept in a green bottle, drifted from the first floor up to him on the third. The two bottles of smells for the house had a wick that looked like a grey tongue. He liked this mixture of smells more that night than in the ten years he had lived in her house. That was the night he bought this very house in which he now stands looking out at his unknown neighbours.

Quietly as the creaking linoleum allowed, he had walked down from his flat to use the bathroom. It was beside the communal kitchen. For ten years he had used caution and was always conscious of the smells and the noise when he was inside that cold room. He always ran the water at full blast to stifle the explosion and the smell. Down the steps of green indoor-outdoor carpeting, then over the thick broadloom leading him to the first floor, where he stood noiselessly inside the screen door of glass and chicken wire. He stared at it through the peephole. His house. It appeared circular, almost round within the restriction of the peep-hole. The house was like a womb. His eyes were watery from the strain of looking. He could hardly breathe. The landlady's television started to play "O, Canada." He waited until the national anthem was over, until the martial music became a hum and then silence. And in that cold white silence he took a last look at his house. The broad-loom changed back into the indoor-outdoor carpeting, he was back again in the area of his flat, linoleum creaking on the uneven stairs. He could hear each step. He did not know until he had reached his flat that he had walked so heavily. He was still wearing his construction boots. And before he closed the door, he laughed aloud. Three doors somewhere in the rooming house opened and he could hear the inquisitive steps into the hallway, then the slam-ming of the doors in disgust. He stared at his wife's worried eyes, and he heard his own laughter and then hers, rejoicing at his success.

He believed she was a religious woman. He believed she was a weak woman. He watched her practise her religion day and night with a Christian silence, as if she was doing it to give him a whipping. He remained at home, shining shoes and airing his suits, when she took her Sunday-morning journeys to the Shaw Street Baptist Church. She wore brown against her brown skin, with the only relief being the glossy silver of her hair. And a string of pearls. And he followed her out of the corner of his eye, out of the right side of the second-floor window, as she set out for the ten blocks to Bloor and Shaw streets.

In his imagination he would follow her down the incline, at which point she always had to slacken her pace because, as she complained after each Sunday, she had "symptoms and pains." It was unbearable to hear her speak this way, as it was when he watched her try to turn the pages of her Bible. Every afternoon when other women would read the *Star*, she read her Bible religiously. And sometimes she read aloud, as if she was telling him a bedtime story. *"The sleep of the labouring man is sweet. . ."*

And he would be on the couch dozing in front of the television, the half-empty glass of Canadian Club at an angle ready to crash on the coffee table, and he would be saved each time by the scoring of a goal and the explosion of noise in the Gardens, and would wake to hear *". . .will not suffer him to sleep."*

"You really miss her, don't ya?" His former landlady was sitting on his verandah. It was a summer afternoon. He was watering his roses. The aluminium chair in which she sat was his wife's favourite.

He was pouring too much water over the chrysanthemums. The water was breaking off their stalks.

"You really miss her."

He washed the mould from his hands and joined her. "How's your nephew?"

"This place's too big. You should move to a smaller place. Even a room. Or back in with me! What you say to that? My nephew's moved out. Sammy. My first sister's first boy. Had to ask him to leave. But he's not far from me. Just over there at Golden Acres on Bathurst. He likes it there." She paused at the end of each piece of information she gave him, as if she wanted him to fill in the rest for himself. He did not know whether she would go on. "That's the best place for someone with his condition.

Cancer, ya know. I can't be bothered looking after him. Too much time and too much work. I have my church, as you know. Keeps me busy. I just had to get him in a nice home. Now he's his own man. But I make him visit me every Saturday. My church keeps me busy all Sunday. This cancer is such a bad thing. A person needs attention all the time. . ."

He was thinking of the broken stems. When this woman left, he would prop them up with sticks. She got up, pulled the part of her dress that was stuck in the crease of her behind, raised her dress high enough for him to see her legs, and prepared to leave. He saw the thick blue veins, like wandering worms in the fat parts inside her knees. "I'll get my nephew to come over and keep you company. He's coming Sunday this time. On Sunday I have to run down to the hospital to visit a church member."

As night closed in and he was into the last fifth of the bottle of rye, feeling the full weight of loneliness which he experienced every night in the summer, at sunset, the same heaviness that he knew so many years ago in Barbados, as if the word "dusk" meant that dark scales or ashes from a nearby fire were falling all around him, he began to do what he always did at this time of night, whether in Toronto or in Barbados. He began to touch things: objects that made him remember brighter times.

He brought his old copies of *Popular Mechanics* from the basement and put them into boxes. Next, he packed his winter boots and the two pairs of old work boots. He threw them back onto the concrete floor of the basement, and with a cigarette dangling at the corner of his mouth, and rye-and-ginger in hand, he went upstairs. The natural light of day and the light in the house was now mixed. At this time of day, when he was a small boy, his mother always asked him to shut the windows in her bedroom, to keep out the mosquitoes. And always, wherever he was, he would enter his bedroom at this time of day, not knowing why, until this Saturday evening when he stood in the bedroom where she died.

The white crocheted bedspread, now turning grey, was as she had left it. Some necklaces of beads, large as red grapes, were on the frame of the mirror on her bureau. Her copies of *The Light of Life, Living a Christian Life* and the *Watchtower* were piled neatly, month by month, on the floor beside the bed. Her embroidery — palm trees growing out of red earth, and two pieces of needlepoint with *God Bless This House* in shaky script — were on the bureau top. Hanging in the clothes cupboard were all her dresses, untouched for eleven months from the day she had ironed them. They now looked like carcasses of slaughtered, undernourished animals. In circular wooden frames, there were other pieces of embroidery, mere outlines, drawn in pencil on cloth. Her winter boots with the fur trimming and woollen balls at the end of the laces stood upright like the two ushers at the funeral parlour. And the monthly *Baptist Messenger*, which she stacked in a neat pile after reading twice.

He was too close to her while he sat on her bed. But he was drawn to her, in a headiness of exciting adventure, as a climber ignores the perils of height for the sake of exploration.

In his hands is the shoe box. In it is her jewellery. When will he hear from the saleswoman? Bright gold-coloured brooches, clusters of luscious fruits and bouquets of flowers. They do not remind him of his gardens in the city parks. Some are silver-painted stars of glittering waterfalls, and buttons and pins given to her with relentless frequency for her attendance at church and her Christian devotion. He puts his hand deeper into the box and fingers her jewellery. When he was a child, at the beach, he used to dig into the soft, wet sand until he reached the water below. Into his grasp came a strand of pearls. He had bought them for her. Was it a birthday or an anniversary? She wore them every Sunday over her brown skin. The skin of the pearls was peeling now. He should have buried her in this necklace.

The long slithering necklace ran through his fingers, like soft sand, bead after peeled bead, and he measured the months of loneliness with each bead.

Her bureau drawers were filled with her underclothes. Some he had never seen before. Her pink corset, its metal stays covered in silk corrugated cloth, was like a rack of ribs in his hands. He threw it back into the drawer, slammed the door and left.

When he sat in his chair, with the white embroidered headrest, a rye in his hand, the television took over his senses and he was soon in a deep sleep.

It was a beautiful morning when he drew the window shades apart. He was in the first-floor living room. He had slept in his work uniform again. The sun came in like a bullet. His spirits were high. He felt vigorous and he added up the things he wanted to do. It was as if he was among his flower beds in the east end park. If only they would approve his transfer soon. . .

Sibelius Park was ablaze with colour and already filled with children. A green Frisbee sailed from one end of his window and disappeared out the other, leaving a rainbow of excitement and children's laughter. His former landlady faced him, coming up the walk. An old man was scraping behind her, his shoes sounding like iron on the cement. He remembered the old man's cancer. He must be walking in pain. He looked terminal inside his oversized suit. But he was smiling.

"Here's Sammy!"

Her nephew's face was red. Did they leave him out in the sun on the verandah over at Golden Acres and forget to take him in?

"Sammy, tell Mr. Trotman about Golden Acres. I won't

be gone a minute. . ." She was already at the end of the walk. "He caught me unawares. I thought he was coming tomorrow. . ."

But he was glad for the company.

Sammy was a silent man. Whenever he had seen him passing and had waved at him, he was smiling and dressed in a three-piece suit which was always too big for him. Did the cancer cause the padding in the shoulders to droop?

Sometimes the pain in his body came over his smiles, like bacteria on a leaf. It seemed to stab him now when he moved his body to take the three steps to reach the door.

They sat without talking, looking out at the park. A pink Frisbee joined the green one. And a dog ran and jumped after it.

"Ya want one of these?" Sammy asked. He turned his head to see Sammy take a short flat brown bottle from inside his breast, unscrew it and put it to his lips. His swallow pipe jumped like a piston, up and down. "Jees!" He passed the back of his hand lightly across his lips. He pressed his lips tightly, and shook his head and squeezed his eyes shut. When he opened them, they had taken on a look of pain, rebuke and fear. "Jees!" he said. His face was washed in a smile.

He left Sammy smiling and went into the kitchen. He returned with glasses, ice, a bottle of ginger ale and a bottle of Canadian Club. A larger smile broke out, like the sun, on Sammy's face. The children in the park were screaming for joy at the elusive Frisbees.

"Jees!" he said again.

They drank the first one in silence.

"The bitch," Sammy said. He took another drink. And with each sip, he did the same thing with his lip, his eyes and his head. The silence returned between them, strong as an old bond. He could see long afternoons of loneliness and few words and deep memories in Sammy's watery eyes.

"Here's to Golden Acres!" Sammy said. "Jees!" His

laughter was a blend of coughing and a splutter. He clapped his chest. "Golden Acres!" His words were like two plates dropped on cement. He held the bottle, and his hand grew tense around its neck, and the blue veins swelled in that hand and became prominent, as if they were about to burst, as if he was about to break the neck of the bottle. "Jees!"

He unscrewed the bottle. After he poured himself a drink, he placed the bottle on the table, and his hands relaxed, and his body relaxed and went almost dead; all feeling went from his face, and the skin looked like sagging layers of leather, his eyes like the circles left by the two glasses of water on the table. He sat like that, his hands dropped to his sides, and breathing heavily. "The bottle," he said, lifting the glass, "and my cigars" — taking a package of White Owls from his pocket — "is the only two things they left me with. Best two things in the world. Keeps me from going mad. Or killing that bitch. Or setting the place on fire."

He did not know if Sammy meant Golden Acres or his aunt's house.

"So you're selling this place!" He put his own bottle of rye into his breast pocket. He forced life out of his body and sat limp, summoning another thought about Golden Acres before taking on the exertion of talking. "You coming to Golden Acres? You coming to be a goddamn inmate like me?" He was dead again.

Sombre and flushed with the rye, he watched Sammy slide almost onto his back, slouched under the weight of his memories and the drink. Sammy sat up, poured a large drink and said, "You sixty yet?"

"Sixty-one," he lied.

"Jees!" Sammy said, and immediately he appeared younger. "Better be going." He seemed very sad now, and resigned. He took something from his other breast pocket and sprayed it into his mouth. "Jees! You're from Jamaica, ain't it?" He sprayed his mouth a second time.

"Barbados."

The smell of peppermint was high in the room long after he left.

The new week began like a Dutch bulb in bloom. His foreman had approved his transfer. And he spent the rest of that Monday morning amongst children and flowers in Sibelius Park. He did not care that they had given him only one helper. He was within sight of his home.

The saleswoman came twice that day with prospective buyers, all of them wealthy even by appearance. But he had now changed his mind about selling the house and was about to tell the saleswoman when she smiled and said, "I'd like a spare key. You shouldn't have to leave your job to let me in."

All that night he drank and went from room to room, pulling the blinds shut as a watchman closes doors. He retraced his steps, room by room, and turned off all the lights except those in her bedroom. He walked around the bed many times, each time crossing his reflection in the oval mahogany mirror on the bureau laden with her beads. He could not conquer the space in the rest of the house, and so he confined himself to the small room, the third-floor bedroom. But he could not sleep.

He went down to the first floor and sat in his favourite chair in the dark. He held the shoe box with her jewellery in his lap. He sat and drank and spent a long time sifting through the box, letting the strand of pearls fall through his fingers, until it slithered to the end where she had attached a silver cross. He had not noticed this before.

When the telephone rang, it was already morning and he was still in the chair, dressed in his green work clothes. The contents of the box were scattered on the floor, but in his hand was the cross.

"Congratulations!"

He did not know what time it was. He did not recognize

the voice. He thought he had just dozed off.

"Good morning!"

The voice was more pleasant now.

"I have a buyer for you."

It was the saleswoman. "We're coming over right away. You have an offer to sign. What a lovely day!"

She arrived just as he was leaving for the park. The buyer came through the door without greeting him, and immediately praised the possibilities of the house. "Great! This wall will come out! The whole wall. I'll townhouse it. These stairs have to go. A winding staircase right here. Right up to the third floor. After I tear out a couple more walls, you know, open it up to let it breathe. . ."

He could feel the dust in his nostrils, and his sinus returning, and he relived the first years of his ownership of the house when this was a working-class street, before it was transformed by renovation trucks, heating trucks, gas-installation trucks, contractors' trucks and garbage trucks.

"How soon can you move out?"

He gave the buyer immediate occupancy.

"The sooner the better," she said.

He could see the line of her brassiere. He could see the line of flesh above her bikini panties. And he could see the complete outline of her panties. They were not the same colour as her light-weight dress. Although he had signed, he still did not like her.

He went back to his park. As he cleaned the garden beds, children threw Frisbees into the air, and some of them landed beside him.

He had cut the last thread of his connection.

He looked up and saw them leaving.

Children walked gingerly in and out of his garden beds at the far corner of the park, and each time a ball or a Frisbee landed, he threw it back to them. The black-and-white soccer ball came to him, and at the last moment it swerved away. *"Pardon!"* As he bent down to kill a worm, he watched a young man stomp on a cluster of Dutch bulbs, trying to pick up a Frisbee. A dog stepped lightly through the bed of chrysanthemums and bent down. But before the thin brown sausage was out of its shivering body, he threw a rake at him.

He looked across the street and saw two vans parked in front of his house. One was marked *Teperman Renovations* and the other *Marvel Landscaping*. Disregarding the rake and the children and the dog, he rushed across the street. He couldn't believe they would come so soon!

The buyer and the saleswoman and the men from the renovations and landscaping companies were walking through rooms, pushing furniture aside, measuring running lines of cord along walls and making small dots with a pencil. He was standing just inside the front door. Their voices came down to him from her bedroom. They did not know he was home. He heard their gleeful voices, and surer, it seemed, than his own fifteen years ago when he acquired the house.

"You got it for a song!"

Their footsteps were over his head.

"I'll take care of your kickback." He recognized the buyer's voice.

"I didn't tell him you were a developer." He recognized her voice.

They were coming down now. She was the first to appear. She saw him standing there and she flashed a smile.

He went back outside. He discovered they had walked through his garden beds. Chalk marks that roads-department men make on sidewalks when they're measuring for sewers were all along his walk.

He had left her memory inside. And he had left her shoe box, and all her clothes, her private accumulation of fifteen years. And now these strangers were drawing lines on the walls of her bedroom and along the floors she had walked so silently and painfully. Their hands had touched her bed. And their footprints were in his flower beds.

He heard the front door bang. The saleswoman was running out behind him. He walked away without answering.

Back in the park, he sat on a bench. Children were all around him.

She came out ahead of the three men. The buyer stood with his hands akimbo. The two workmen shook hands and drove off. She left in her silver-grey BMW. Only the buyer remained. He moved from one side of the house to the other, bending down at basement windows, all the time jotting things in a book. At last he left. But he saw him come back in a black Cadillac, drive slowly up to the house, stop, and then move on. He passed beside him sitting on the bench.

A dog was at his feet, licking his construction boots. It was the same dog he had chased earlier. The dog came closer and sat between his boots.

As the warmth went out of the day and the children ran home, as if a bell of hunger and obedience had summoned them, he was left alone in the park with the dog still sitting between his muddy boots. The flowers seemed to make one last shiver before the night air bent them slightly for their long sleep. All around him lights came on in houses, but he remained sitting there, motionless in the large sea of grass as the park seemed to turn into a lake and he was anchored to the bench which moved only with his imagination.

Sammy would already be in his room for the night, with a bottle of rye under his pillow for company and warmth.

He could no longer see his house, for it had become submerged in the same darkness in which he and the dog sat. But he imagined it was still there.

The shoe box was all he would take to his new place, whether that place was the rooming house or Golden Acres.

The dog jumped up beside him on the green bench and put its head between his legs.

Shapes moved in the windows on the border of the park. The dog nudged closer to him to say good night with a warm licking tongue, or good-bye, and was soon lost in the darkness. His eyes followed its first trotting steps in the shadows and then could not find it among the trees and the toolshed.

He got up and collected his tools and took them into the shed. He walked to the far corner of the park where his helper had left the lawn mower; he rolled it backwards and locked it up. He walked the few dark yards to his house, but when he stood in front of it and saw its own darkness and absence of life, he turned away and walked instead to Bathurst Street. He bought a bottle of ginger ale, a bottle of Canadian Club and some cigarettes. He went along Bathurst, just walking and thinking, until he found himself beside Golden Acres. The entire building was ablaze with fluorescent lights. He wished he knew which was Sammy's room. He walked to the front door, past the nurse sitting at a desk reading the *Star*. "You're getting in rather late," she said.

He was climbing the stairs, looking into empty rooms where the lights were fierce as in the lobby. In one, there was an old man motionless on a small white bed. In another, an old woman was sitting upright on a white sheet and her lips were moving. There was no other sign of life on that floor. He walked along another corridor, hearing only his construction boots on the grey linoleum, until he reached the top floor. It was noiseless there too. He retraced his steps. On the way out, the nurse looked up and nodded and said, "Oh, you're just visiting. . ."

He was back on the bench in the park. The dog had not returned. He opened the door of the toolshed. The bulb in the small cement room was weak and he tripped among

172

the hoses. He moved some tools aside and some snakes of hoses and forks before he found the can which contained gas for the lawn mower. He filled an empty bottle and left. He walked slowly with the three bottles, ginger ale, rye and gas.

He entered his house and left the front door wide open. He turned on the lights in each room, right up to the third floor. He went back to the kitchen and poured himself a rye-and-ginger, and sat with the shoe box on the kitchen table. The house was quiet. The house was bright. He had missed Sammy's room. Perhaps it was the one in darkness.

He took the bottle with the gas back to the third floor, and just as he would do with plant fertilizer in his own garden or in the park, he sprinkled the gas around the edges of the rooms, one room at a time, some on the bed, some on the white crocheted doilies she had made, all down the stairs to the first floor. He doused the kitchen and the bathroom more lavishly, more carefully, as if he was coaxing young plants. He washed his hands under the cold-water tap with Sunlight soap. It felt as if small snakes or worms were pulling at his skin, as if his skin was tightening.

Now he could not find his cigarettes. He could not find his matches. He didn't know which floor to light first. He hadn't thought about that. Should he light the third floor, and then run down to the second, and then the first, and then run outside and go back to the shed which he had forgotten to lock? In twenty years he had never been so careless.

He took another drink. He always had to take a second drink to help him unknot a problem. The cigarettes and matches were on the table. The shoe box was hiding them. Was she in the room with him? She was always there to tell him where he had misplaced his cigarettes. She was always so careful!

He lit the cigarette. He threw the match into the sink. He got up with the shoe box and his drink. And immediately, as the glass touched his lips, so too did the flames kiss the gas and fly up and engulf him; and before he could think of where the front door was, the explosion came.

He could not move. He could not see. He could not cry out. There was no smoke. Only the orange of fire, bright as the colours of spring in the park. And the last thing he heard, or thought he heard, was the terrified yelping of a dog, arrived too late, scampering from the rage of the fire.

About the Author

Austin Chesterfield Clarke has enjoyed a distinguished academic career, teaching at Yale University, Duke University, Williams College, the University of Texas at Austin and the University of Western Ontario. In addition, he served as Cultural Attaché to the Barbados Embassy in Washington, D.C., from 1974 to 1976.

Austin Clarke is best known, however, for his prodigious output of short stories and novels. He has published eight books, including the trilogy *The Meeting Point, Storm of Fortune* and *The Bigger Light*. He has been acclaimed for his sensitive portrayal of the problems of West Indian immigrants.

Austin Clarke is currently living in Toronto.